SECRETS
FOR SALE

Also by Jerri Kay Lincoln:

Rutledge Historical Society Cozy Mysteries
Message for Murder
Death over Divorce
Kousins Kan't Kill
Rogues to Riches
Secrets for Sale
Lady Smith Lady

Memoir
The Dog Who Rescued Me

Children's Books
Sparkles the Unicorn and Kindness
Cooper's Smile
The Little Unicorn Who Could
Do Bears Poop in the Woods?
Can Pigs Fly?
Why Do Puppy Dogs Have Cold Noses?
The Invisible Lion
La Petite Licorne Qui Pouvait
Das Kleine Einhorn Was Es Kann
The Little Unicorn Who Could Coloring Book
Do Bears Poop in the Woods? Coloring Book

Cookbooks
Ten Delicious Dairy-Free Stevia-Sweetened Ice Cream Recipes

Secrets for Sale

Jerri Kay Lincoln

Ralston Store Publishing
P.O. Box 1684
Prescott, Arizona 86302

ISBN 978-1-938322-58-7

The reader should note that the nutritional beliefs and food choices in this book are those of the characters and not necessarily those of the author or publisher.

Dedicated to the sleuth in all of us.

CHAPTER ONE

THE RUTLEDGE, ARIZONA High Council meeting room was at the end of a long hallway lined with pictures of various types of cacti. Although I had been in the building several times visiting my boss, Martha Goldstein, I had never been inside the council meeting room. At my feet my dog, Bingo, a Cavalier King Charles Spaniel, leaned against me. Since I'd gotten him *back*, he went almost everywhere with me.

Petra Hamilton, the sixteen-year-old girl whom I worked with, sat next to me. I shouldn't say girl, I should call her a woman. Weird, yes, but a woman. Petra wore her hair cut short —her purple hair, that is—and had tattoos and piercings all over her face and other body parts. That's what I've heard, anyway. I'd only seen the piercings on her face; and oh, yeah, I've seen the bellybutton ring when she wears those short blouses that I still can't believe the high school allows. In my day, the dress code—wait, you probably don't want to hear about that.

Sitting on the other side of Petra was her boyfriend, Mason. He was a tattooed-up biker. Don't think I'm judging these two. I used to, yes. I've learned that lesson—okay, okay, I'm still learn-ing that lesson—but these two are awesome. Mason was in pre-med in Flagstaff, and Petra was in a special program to complete her last two years of high school and her first two years of col-lege simultaneously. The school only offers that opportunity to the best and brightest. And Petra is all that and more. She is also

1

responsible, reliable, and conscientious. I can't say enough good about Petra, but I've probably said enough already, so I'll shut up for now.

When I sat down, Petra leaned over and whispered to me, "There he is. The one who plans to buy the Rutledge Historical Society building." She motioned with her head to the front row on the other side of the room. Two men, father and son, sat there looking quite satisfied with themselves—at least the father did. The son looked uncomfortable.

I glanced around, searching the faces of the audience. Besides the two men in the front, and Petra, Mason, and I, there were only three other people in attendance. When I came again to the two in the front row, the father turned around and made eye contact. I glared at him; and the jerk smiled, like he had it all and there was nothing I could do about it. And that was mostly true. But I was here to change things.

There were six rows of five chairs each on either side of the aisle in the section of the room reserved for the audience. The padded chairs, covered with black corduroy, were surprisingly comfortable. The face I searched for was nowhere in sight. That face was Billy Madrigal, my husband. *Sheriff* Billy Madrigal. And my *new* husband! We hadn't even been married a week yet, but because the wedding was quick and unexpected—no, it wasn't because of that. Get your mind out of the gutter—we hadn't gone on our honeymoon yet.

The honeymoon was also delayed because of this meeting, which I had to attend. The town council, in all their short-sightedness and lack of wisdom, decided to sell the Rutledge Historical Society building, where Petra and I worked. That's why Petra and I were here.

I'll be honest with you. I don't need to work. That is, I don't need to work *financially*. But there are other needs besides financial needs, right? And my need is that I am absolutely and positively not the country club, golf, and luncheon with the hoity-toity ladies sort of person. Kill me now, please. That is not my thing. And I enjoyed working at the historical society.

I heard heavy footsteps of cowboy-booted feet and turned around to see Billy walk in the door. He winked at me and sat on the other side of the aisle. He had already told me he wouldn't sit next to me because he was afraid I would make a spectacle of myself, and he didn't want to taint the distinguished office of the sheriff. Yes, he really said that, but he was joking. Wasn't he? I think he was. He smiled when he said it, I think.

The audience's soft conversations ebbed as several members of the council walked in and seated themselves. I didn't know most of them, although I recognized the mayor, Joe Stoddard, the vice-mayor, Christa Hawthorne, who owned a little boutique just down from the historical society, and two of the council members: Anthony Petrelli, owner of a used and new car lot, and Paul Gallagher, vice-principle of the high school. The mayor sat in the middle, with the vice-mayor, on his right. I guess Christa was his right-hand man. Or something. The three remaining council members sat on the other side of the mayor. Perpendicular to the seven-person panel was a two-person desk at each end. Martha Goldstein sat at the left desk and a man I didn't know sat at the right desk.

I leaned over to Petra. "So Martha is on the town council? I didn't realize that."

"Lorry!" she said in her condescending voice I tried to ignore, "No, she's not on the council! Martha is the town manager! Why can't you remember that?"

"It's not that I forgot it, Petra, I thought she was the town clerk."

Petra shook her head in disgust and whispered something to Mason that made him lean forward, glance at me, and laugh. I ignored that, too.

"Who is that person on the right, across from Martha?"

"That's Russell Tabor. *He's* the town clerk."

Paul Gallagher and Anthony Petrelli sat to the right of Christa Hawthorne. "Petra, who are the three people to the left of the mayor?"

"Left to right, Brent Lindsay, Elizabeth Conroy, and Douglas Gates."

Now it was my turn to be haughty. "Petra! I can see by their nameplates what their names are! What I don't know is who they are!"

"Brent Lindsay owns the Rutledge Super Market. Rumor had it Douglas Gates was related to Bill Gates and his fortune. Elizabeth Conroy is the retired principal of the high school. Wasn't she the principal when you attended school there?"

"Now that you mention it, the name sounds familiar." I had been back in Rutledge almost a year and still had a lot to learn. Not that I had just moved to town—I grew up here. But I went away to college and returned not quite a year ago. Since then, my life had gone through some miraculous changes. I'd tell you about them, but the meeting was about to start.

Before it did, Petra leaned over and said one more thing to me, a catch in her voice. "I know she was there when my brother was in school."

Petra didn't talk about her brother too often. She rarely mentioned him—which I could understand, because I had lost a sibling, too.

The mayor pounded his gavel in front of him and said, "I'd like to call the meeting to order. Rise with me, please, for the pledge of allegiance." He put his hand on his heart and pivoted around facing the flag on the wall behind him. There were three flags behind him, though, the United States flag, the Arizona flag, and the Rutledge County flag with the town seal on it. The town seal showed a baby javelina with a smile on its cute, little face. It looked like the mayor was facing the Rutledge flag. Maybe he just liked javelinas. Although, it was difficult to tell which flag since they were all so close together.

Everyone in the audience stood up, put their hands on their hearts, and recited in unison with the High Council. The reason —the stupid reason—the Town Council calls themselves the High Council is because Jacob High, from the late nineteenth century, was instrumental in founding the town. The Rutledge

Historical Society building, in all its splendor and glory, stood on High Street—also named after Jacob High. But for the town council, after all these years, to still call themselves the High Council, seemed a little silly and pompous to me. With a name like that, they should all wear party hats or something.

At the end of the pledge, the mayor and the rest of the council turned around and sat down. The mayor said, "Thank you and welcome." He looked over at Russell Tabor. "Can we have a roll call, please?"

Tabor, a thin, gangly sort of man, nodded without smiling and started calling off names of everyone on the council, prefacing each one with "Council Member" until he got to the mayor and vice-mayor. As he called each person's name, they responded with "Here" or "Yes." It was more mindless bureaucratic non-sense that I knew I would get an overload of on this night. I hoped I could say my piece, they would change their minds about selling the historical society because of the lucidity and brilliance of my arguments, and that would be the end of it. But that's not always how things turn out, is it?

There was a lightness to the meeting, a feeling of jocularity and bonhomie I didn't feel. If they knew how I felt, the meeting wouldn't have that feeling to it at all. Apparently, no one had told them. I was a little concerned Billy might—since he was the sheriff and a respected member of the Rutledge officials and all —but when he told me he didn't plan on sitting with me, I knew then that he hadn't said a word. The so-called High Council wasn't sitting in wait for me to explode on them, and that was good. Surprise is a wonderful thing. If they don't expect my passionate speech, I might even make a difference and get my way. I liked getting my own way. Who doesn't?

There was even more bureaucratic nonsense going on that I tuned out. Motion this and motion that. It was like a game I played when I was a kid. Too bad the game was so boring I didn't even remember its name. The white noise in the back-ground of the room—it was white noise *to me*, anyway—gave me time to reminisce about what had happened to me in the past several months.

I had left an abusive marriage, gotten a divorce—well, almost, then it turned out I didn't need one—gotten a good job, adopted my son, met and married an amazing man, and last and definitely not least, I had inherited my mother's gazillions. When she died, her attorneys lied to me saying that she had given it all to charity. Then I started going over the murders that had happened in Rutledge since I returned to town when Petra poked me with her elbow.

"You're up," she said. "You have one minute. Don't waste it."

I had heard through the white noise haze of the meeting they had said something about a call to the public and going to the podium. So I stood up and strolled my big butt up to the podium right past the father and son *usurpers* in the front row. While I would have liked to have farted in their faces as I walked by, that particular option wasn't available to me at that precise moment, if you know what I mean.

All right, I have to admit something you would find out in a minute, anyway. I'm not much of a public speaker. It's never been something I have aspired to or found much interest in. And I didn't practice or plan what I would say in the meeting. I figured my passion would carry me through. Well, it didn't.

When I glanced at Martha and Billy, neither of them looked at me. I think they expected the worst. And they should have. Very respectfully, I nodded to the mayor and the council. "Mayor, council, I can't believe you idiots are really trying to sell the historical society building! Don't you realize how many people enjoy going to see the exhibits every year?"

The audience and the council erupted in pandemonium with my first statement, so I don't think they even heard the more important question that followed it. Bingo, besieged with me at the podium, looked at me nervously.

The mayor pounded his gavel, scowled at Billy, and said, "Sheriff Madrigal. Can't you keep your wife in order?"

"Obviously not," said Billy with a straight face. "You're welcome to try."

The audience exploded in laughter, and I even saw some sly smiles on the members of the council. Even the mayor had to suppress a laugh. "Lorry Madrigal, that is enough. You are excused. Is there anyone else who would like to address the council?"

"Lockharte," I said.

"What?" asked the mayor, clearly annoyed.

"Lockharte. My last name is Lockharte. I kept my maiden name. I'm not Lorry Madrigal, I'm Lorry Lockharte."

The mayor waved me away with the back of his hand and repeated, "Anyone else?"

As I held my head high and strolled back to my seat acting like I had been eloquent instead of atrocious, Petra stood up and walked to the podium. Instead of her usual loud and questionable attire, she wore a conservative black skirt and light blue blouse. I thought maybe she could charm them and get across to them what I had hoped to and miserably failed at.

My hopes crumbled when Petra reached the podium because there were giggles and jeers from the audience. Although she was dressed conservatively, she couldn't hide her purple hair, tattoos, and piercings. Didn't Petra get the last giggle, though! When she began to speak in a clear, authoritative tone, with all the eloquence I wanted but didn't have, the audience silenced themselves and listened.

"My name is Petra Hamilton. I have worked part time at the Rutledge Historical Society for the past two years. In that time, I have watched small children grow excited over the exhibits, while their parents marveled at the history that drew them inside. And hidden between the covers of our genealogical binders, I have seen people discover secrets about their family that surprised and delighted them. We are in the process of scanning all our documents so the records will be available online. Are you really going to sell off the Rutledge Historical

Society building and let all that history—the history of *our* town —go to waste? Are you—"

But she didn't get to finish because the mayor said, "That's all the time you have, Miss Hamilton. Take your seat, please."

That's when I realized what was happening. They didn't want to hear it. They had already made up their minds, and it was a done deal. The thought made me sick to my stomach. When Petra sat down beside me, I whispered to her, "You did great."

She whispered back, "A lot of good it did. They've already made up their minds."

Petra and I thought alike. That was scary. The whole event depressed me, and I would have stood up and walked out of the place in disgust, but when I glanced over at Billy, he narrowed his eyes at me disapprovingly. So I kept my seat.

The next item at the meeting was called a consent agenda. Russell Tabor, the town clerk, read a bunch of items off. Then the mayor said, "Is there anything you want pulled from the consent agenda to be considered and discussed separately?"

Everyone said, "Not me," or something like that. The mayor said, "Will someone make a motion to accept the consent agenda?"

That shocked me from my silence. I stood up and blurted out, "Is that what happened to the historical building? It was on some agenda and never even discussed? No one in town even knew—"

The mayor pounded his gavel. "Mrs. Madri—Lockharte! You are out of order! Sit down now!" He glared at me, and I shrank under his gaze and took my seat.

Someone on the council said, "I make a motion to accept the consent agenda."

Someone else said, "I second it."

The mayor said, "All in favor say, aye."

Everyone on the council said, "Aye," and when they finished, the mayor said, "Any opposed, say nay." I was about to stand up again in protest and nay my brains out until Petra put her hand over my mouth. It was probably a good thing.

The mayor said, "Motion carried." Then he added, "Council may vote to recess public meeting for ten minutes and hold an executive session for discussion and consultation with the town attorney regarding contract negotiations."

Again, someone made the motion and someone else seconded it. The mayor did the all-in-favor thing again, everyone said aye and no one said nay. So the mayor said, "Motion carried. Ten-minute recess before we begin the executive session."

The entire town council stood as one and scattered to parts unknown. And the jocularity continued as if it had never ended. Apparently, my outbursts hadn't disrupted the general geniality of the council. I wasn't sure if that was good or bad.

Not knowing what would happen after the recess—would the regular town council reconvene after the executive session or was that part finished for the night—I stood up when the rest of the audience stood.

Petra turned to me and said, "Mason and I are leaving, Lorry. We've done all we could, and now we just have to accept the inevitable."

Mason turned to me, grinned, waved, and took Petra's hand. They walked toward the door but stopped before they got there, and Mason turned her around and kissed her. It wasn't just a peck on the lips, this was a complete long-lasting passionate kiss. I didn't think it was a prudent thing to do in front of the council and the general public. Petra was only sixteen years old. It made me wonder if they were *doing it* or not. Honestly, I didn't want to know. Oh, wait. Yes, I did. Curiosity and all that. Wasn't that human nature? You know, wanting to know that sort of thing? Whatever.

So intent was I in watching the Petra and Mason show, that when I turned back around, almost everyone in the room had gone. Several people walked out the door right in front of where Mason and Petra were kissing, but they were all a blur, like when a camera is out of focus.

Billy was talking to Wichita Wiggins, who had been the sheriff when Billy became a deputy and was now the town attorney.

Mayor Joe Stoddard walked in the door and up to Billy and Wichita. He must have walked out along with most everyone else as I watched Mason and Petra. How *long* were they kissing, anyway? As much as I didn't want to talk to the mayor, I wasn't going to stand there alone on the fringes while I waited for Billy. We planned on going home together—maybe not in the same vehicle, but *together*. So I marched my butt up to the three of them, said a warm hello to Wichita, and blatantly ignored the mayor.

He was about to turn to me and say something—I knew that because his body was in motion toward me and his mouth was open—when we heard it. A shot. Bingo gave one short crisp bark. Billy and I and Wichita looked at one another in disbelief, and the mayor said, "That was *loud* for a car backfire."

A second later, without saying a word, Billy bolted out the door in the direction the shot came from.

CHAPTER TWO

"WHAT'S WITH HIM?" asked the mayor. "He in the market for a broken-down used car or something?" He laughed at his own joke.

"Mayor," said Wichita, "with all due respect, sir, that was a gunshot, not a car backfire!"

I knew Wichita well enough to know he would have liked to add some expletives in there, so he had great restraint in not doing so. The mayor, meanwhile, had a look of astonishment on his face, but all he could say was, "Oh." Then he hurried out the door after Billy.

Wichita nodded toward me and hobbled after the mayor with his cane clunking beside him. He was in his sixties, with a stocky build and a balding head sparsely covered in gray hair. His cane wasn't a sign of infirmity—he had broken his ankle hang gliding with his grandchildren. When his ankle healed, he could probably participate in the Olympics and be competitive. The man was tough and had heart. The Town of Rutledge had lured him back to town after he moved back East to be closer to his grandchildren. But when the council offered him a job as town attorney, he couldn't turn it down.

People had started filtering back into the room looking confused. I would have critically examined each one individually to see who might be the murderer, but I didn't know yet if there was a murder. Knowing my history since I moved to Rutledge, though—well, let's put it this way: since I moved back to town, Rutledge had become the murder capital of Arizona. Maybe the United States. Maybe the world. No, maybe not that bad. So considering that history, I looked over each person who came in so I could check them off the list of who might have been shot.

It wasn't Martha, thank goodness, as she was sitting at her desk kneading her hands and looking worried. It wasn't Russell Tabor, because he was at his desk shuffling papers and looking unconcerned. Hmmm. That might be suspicious. But since I didn't know if or who had been murdered, I couldn't rule him in or out. You know how it is: no motive, no murder.

Petra and Mason should have been long gone before we heard the shot, I hoped. Although, since they were together, there would have been two shots, so I didn't think it was either of them. Several members of the council were back at their places. They had nameplates in front of them, but I was too busy to look. Who was missing? I didn't see the wicked man. Wait! There was his son straining his neck looking around the room presumably for his father.

I examined the room carefully. The whole council was there except the mayor, but it couldn't have been him. None of the audience had returned, so all of them were unaccounted for. The aforementioned wicked man was not in attendance.

Before I had a chance to ponder that, the mayor returned, stood to the side, and elevated his voice so the whole room could hear. "Everyone, I have to report a murder." He looked over to the son. "Todd, someone has shot your father. I'm so sorry."

Todd stood up, looked around, and sat back down. "Murdered? Who would murder my father?" He stood up again and looked around the room, his eyes settling on me.

The mayor, who couldn't tell a gunshot from a car backfire, was a little more adept at reading people, thankfully. "No, Todd, it wasn't her. She was with me when it happened."

The rest of the council murmured their condolences, but Todd didn't seem to hear. He stood back up, scowled at me, and fled out the door without saying another word.

My first thought was: yes, his performance looked convincing. But doesn't he inherit the entire company? Money is always a motive for murder.

Meanwhile, the entire council had stood up. The two women, Christa Hawthorne and Elizabeth Conroy, were weeping and hugging the men and each other. Martha looked distressed but didn't stand up to join in the group hugs. And Russell Tabor sat there watching. He was a strange man, and he was already on my list of suspects.

The council sat down again, and with his head down and his shoulders stooped, the mayor walked slowly to his seat. He took the gavel in his hand, but instead of pounding it, he laid it down in front of him. And then he spoke. "Considering what's just happened, there is no need for an executive session for contract negotiations right now." He looked up and out at the audience, which consisted of just li'l ole me. "And our attorney isn't even here now—not that it matters. We may or may not have business with Fenton and Son Incorporated—through Todd Fenton—but we will have to wait for another day to ascertain that. We're done for today." The mayor picked up the gavel, gave a light tap on the desk in front of him, and set it back down.

I think in all the excitement he forgot all about that first motion, second motion, motion carried business, because the rest of the council looked at him expectantly. He sat there with his head down and didn't say a word. Then he picked his head up and said. "I apologize for any inconvenience it might cause the council, the town manager, and the town clerk"—he nodded toward Martha and Russell Tabor—"but Billy and Wichita have locked the doors to the building, and all of you will be detained for an interview and whatnot."

Since I had heard the shot and now had it confirmed, I knew that *whatnot* would undoubtedly include GSR testing. GSR testing, for those of you innocents out there, was gunshot residue. Sad to say I had personal experience with GSR testing, and it wasn't a good memory. So I'll skip that for now. But the council was in for a surprise if they think whatnot is just finger-printing.

Elizabeth Conroy, or was it Christa Hawthorne, my eye was on my watch and my mind was elsewhere, but a woman's voice that wasn't Martha's said, "What about Todd? He just walked out of here."

"Like I said, all the doors are locked. Nobody is going in or out. He'll be stopped at the door. The only door that can reach the outside is the emergency door, and Wichita has that one covered. Todd'll be back and will have to go through the same interview process as the rest of us.

"The only ones who are not suspects are me, Wichita, and Lorry Lockharte, because the three of us were talking to the sheriff when the shot occurred. We still have to attend the interview to see if we remember who was in the audience right before the recess."

The council spoke softly among themselves, but none of them spoke a word of dissension because they were all good little boys and girls who always went along with authority. Can you tell I'm a little cynical about that? Well, all of them went along with authority except for the one who killed Mr. Fenton. That would be stretching it a little.

"You're all welcome to wander around the room. Unfortunate-ly, though, you cannot use the restroom right now."

Yup, of course not. Because a person can wash off GSR.

"So those of you who, um, have to go, make yourselves known to Sheriff Billy when he returns, and he will interview you first."

The council was a little incensed at not being able to use the restrooms, but again, they kept their animosity to themselves. Like good little boys and girls and all that.

Then the mayor stood unceremoniously and walked toward me. "Lorry, unless there are people who need to use the restroom, Billy said he would interview you first so you could go home. But he didn't say if you needed a ride. So I will take you home after he interviews me," he said authoritatively—like I wasn't supposed to argue.

That's not my way. "Thank you, mayor, but—"

He interrupted me. "I insist. It's the right thing to do. I absolutely will not take no for an answer."

He was a man not used to people standing up to him. "Mayor, you have to. I have my own car. Billy and I were planning to drive home together—in separate cars." He shook his head like he had water in his ears, but I guess it meant he didn't understand. So I tried to explain. "Billy likes to escort me home when I drive my own car."

This time the mayor screwed up his face and shook his head. "So he turns on his lights and siren and follows you home?"

If there wasn't such a somber mood in the place, I would have laughed in his face. As it was, I had to clench my teeth to keep from giggling. "Um, no. He just follows me. No lights or siren."

The mayor nodded and didn't say a word. His comment got me to thinking. It would be cool if Billy turned on his lights when he followed me home. No sirens, though. I wouldn't want to make a spectacle of myself.

CHAPTER THREE

THE MAYOR WALKED back to the panel where the rest of the council members sat quietly conversing among themselves, and I sat down close to the door and tried to make myself unobtrusive, which was no easy feat for me. I *ain't no* ninety-eight-pound weakling. And if you want to know what poundage I do carry, too bad. It's not polite to ask that of a grown woman. Didn't your mother teach you any manners? And don't correct my English, either. I said *ain't* and the *no* for effect.

Todd Fenton tromped through the door, glared at me, and walked up behind the panel where the mayor was sitting. He was about to say something, but Christa got up to hug him, then Elizabeth, then a couple of the men stood up and patted him on the back as they nodded their heads. Todd leaned over and said something to the mayor. I couldn't hear what the mayor answered, but Todd used his hands a lot and ended by shaking a finger at the mayor. Then—I still couldn't hear the conversation and can't read lips, but this was obvious—the mayor put his hands out in front of him, palms up, and leaned slightly forward, while saying, "There's nothing I can do."

Todd stomped his feet back to his seat in the front row, crossing his arms and looking angry. I looked at Martha, but she wouldn't make eye contact. She wasn't only my boss; she was also a good friend. And I had probably embarrassed her with my outburst. Ah, well, she knows me well and knows how important the historical society is to me. What did she expect? For me to just lay down and let the town tramp all over me? I don't think so!

And Russell Tabor sat there in his white shirt, his gray slacks —I couldn't see them under the desk but had noticed when he walked in—and his spit-polished shoes. He still looked guilty.

The rest of the council kept their seats, didn't talk much to the others, and looked tired. It wasn't late, but sitting there like that was boring. BOR-ING! I yawned in their direction to show them it was perfectly okay to do in public as long as you had good reason. And we all had good reason. Where was Billy, anyway? How long does it take for forensics to finish? Billy's deputy, Nick, would do that, anyway. And how long does it take for the medical examiner to arrive? They were only coming from Coyote Moon—formerly known as West Rutledge—the next town over.

I felt bored out of my three-inch heels, but I slipped them back on in case I had to make a run for it. One never knows. Looking around the room because I had nothing else to do, I started with the floor under my heels. It was that same fake hardwood floor as they had in the entryway and down the hallway I had noticed the first time I came here to see Martha. It didn't look real, but maybe I was being too hard on it. Maybe it wasn't supposed to look real. The walls were an off-white with no decorations except one of those three-piece pictures in separate frames. It was a picture of three different kinds of cactus with the same background, and it looked cool.

My observations ended when Petra and Mason came through the door, holding hands, and jabbering. When they saw me sitting at the back, they sat down on either side of me. "What are you guys doing here?" I asked. "Couldn't Billy have interviewed you over the phone to see if you remember who was here?"

Mason, sitting to my right, farthest from the door, leaned over and said, "We're suspects!" He looked proud.

I was waiting for the punch line, but when it didn't come, I broke out in laughter, anyway. "You two? Suspects? Gimme a break!"

Petra put her hands on her hips and said, "What! You don't think I'm capable of being a suspect? I can be a killer as much as anyone else!" Mason and I both tried to hush her down, because everyone in the room had turned their heads toward us. She didn't speak loudly, so I don't think they could hear, but I'm sure they could feel the rancor in her voice. I knew I could.

"No, Petra, it's just—" but I didn't get to finish because Billy appeared at the door, took two steps toward us and whispered, "Lor, I know I said I'd interview you first, but Mason has to get back to Flag. Do you mind? It may take a while. He's a suspect." Flag was what the locals called Flagstaff.

"Yeah, I just heard, and no, I don't mind. Go ahead."

He threw me a kiss, motioned Mason to follow, and stepped out the door. Mason stood up, squeezed in front of me with his backside toward me, made a grunting noise, turned around to me and said, "There. That feels better already."

As he walked away, I figured out what he was talking about. What do they call those?

Petra knew, because she started fanning her hand in front of her face, an action I followed with enthusiasm. "Phew!" she said. "He is *good* at those silent but deadly ones!"

When the stench abated, somewhat, and Petra buried her head in the schoolbook she had brought with her, I began to think about Petra and Mason being suspects. Surely Petra had a motive. She loved working at the historical society as much as I did, probably more. If not for it, she'd be stuck at home with her no-account drunk father sleeping off another hangover. She only worked part time but spent all day at the society studying her courses on the computer. While it was true that if they sold the building it would disrupt Petra's life, I didn't think she would *murder* someone over it. I didn't think she had ever held a gun in her life.

And Mason! While he was Petra's champion and would defend her to the last, he was a gentle soul who was in school to become a doctor. *First, do no harm* and all that. Mason wouldn't harm a fly.

So with that in mind, I didn't think it would take long to eliminate him as a suspect. But he was in with Billy for almost an hour. Mason did have a habit of going on and on when he was with Billy, though, so that probably had something to do with it.

When he finally returned to the council room, he still looked bright and happy. He leaned over, gave Petra a quick kiss, said, "I'll see ya this weekend, babe, and talk to you tomorrow." Then he swiveled his head toward me. "See ya later, Lor." And with that he strode off, wearing his signature jean jacket with Greek letters and looking every bit the bad tattooed biker I had originally thought he was.

CHAPTER FOUR

BILLY APPEARED AT the door a short time later and looked at me. "You can go first, Petra," I said. "I don't mind."

"I'm in the middle of a chapter, Lorry. You can go. But would you mind waiting and taking me home?"

"Not at all, Petra. I'd be happy to." I walked past her and into the hall with Billy. He took me into his arms and gave me a quick hug and kiss. Then he took me and Bingo, who had followed me, into Martha's office. I sat down by the desk and looked at Billy. "Aren't you afraid that you'll get the fingerprint ink all over Martha's desk?"

Billy smiled and held up something that looked like my Kindle. "No more ink! How cool is that?"

"Oh, cool! Can I do it?" I held out my hand.

"Lorry, I already have your fingerprints, and it's getting late. I have to do all those people in there, and I'll probably be here all night. Do you really want your new husband to spend the *entire* night away from his new bride?" He winked at me.

I pulled my hand back into my lap and felt guilty for even asking. "No, new husband."

That made him smile, and he reached out and picked up a legal pad and a pen. "So do you remember anyone from the audience?"

"The only people I knew besides Mason and Petra were the guys buying the building. No one else."

"You're sure?"

I nodded. "Positive. No one. I didn't know half the council, either. Petra had to fill me in."

Billy looked tired already, and his night was just beginning. "All right. You're free to go. Can you send Petra in? It will take longer with her because I have to do her fingerprints. But this machine is quicker than the old variety." He stood up, leaned across the desk, and kissed me lightly on the lips. "Love you, darling. Don't wait up."

I walked out of the room and yawned. Billy's fatigue had attached itself to me. While I would have liked to wait up for him like a dutiful wife—I wasn't a dutiful wife, but I would have liked to have been, I think—it was getting later every second, and it had been a long day.

Most of it I had spent walking back and forth down the hall spewing my angst over the impending sale and having Petra try to quiet me down so she could get her work done. Her efforts were in vain. Now I wished I would have practiced my speech, or at least tried to prepare a speech, so I wouldn't have made such a fool of myself up there. It didn't matter anymore, though. The buyer was dead. His son may or may not want to go through with the sale. But nothing would happen until Billy found the guy's killer. So I had some time to come up with another plan. And somewhere in the back of my mind, I thought it might be a good one.

When I reached the door of the council room, Petra was already on her feet. "I heard you coming," she said. "I recognized the sound of your heels and of Bingo's claws on the floor."

"You had enough practice listening to me walk back and forth down the hallway today!"

"Something like that. See ya soon."

Sitting down again at the back of the room, I pretended I didn't see Todd Fenton glaring at me. Thank goodness I had been in sight of Billy *and* the mayor when the shot killed Todd's father. If not for that, I'm sure I would have been the prime suspect, and with good reason after my outpouring of anger during the council meeting. The finger of suspicion would have pointed my way, but fate had intervened. Obviously—at least obvious to me—it meant I had to help solve the case.

Yes, I had told Billy I would *try* to stop getting involved in murder cases. But *try* was the salient word. He wanted me to promise, but I knew myself better than that. So I sat in the back and tried to analyze every person on the town council. I eliminated Martha as a suspect, because she was, you know, Martha. But I included Russell Tabor, and he was still near the top of my list. Todd Fenton was on the list and also near the top.

Then I would look at the rest of the council, close my eyes, and try to imagine them holding a gun. It was a weird exercise and produced weird results. All the men except Russell Tabor held the gun without compunction.

I would have thought the two women, Christa and Elizabeth, would have looked out-of-place with a gun in their hands. But in my mind's eye, they both looked more than comfortable. They looked capable. Both of them. Eager, even. What were their motives? If only I had been at the first meeting when they discussed selling the building. Then I would know who voted for it and who voted against it. The motive for this murder had to do with the building. That much was obvious. And if the murderer wasn't me, then it had to be one of them. *Which* one of them was the question.

CHAPTER FIVE

"THAT FINGERPRINT DEVICE was cool! Didn't you think so?" Petra remained standing. She was as eager to get home as I was.

I moved my lips into a pout. "Billy wouldn't let me do it. He said he already had my fingerprints, and he didn't have time."

"Well, maybe another time. Who did you say?" she whispered to me.

"What do you mean?" I asked.

"You know, who did you say you thought did it?"

"Billy didn't ask me that. Who did you say?"

She laughed. "I said I thought you did it."

I stood up indignantly. "Petra! Why would you say such a thing?"

"Because it made perfect sense. You were the one who was outraged about the council selling the building. And you were the one who made a spectacle of yourself in front of more than a dozen witnesses. Everything pointed to you."

"Except, Billy must have told you I was with him *and* the mayor when the guy was shot. Color me innocent, Petra."

"Yeah, Billy told me that, but I said you probably had arranged it like that." She smiled and winked, and I didn't know if she was kidding or not.

"Let's go," she said, "unless you want to hang in this boring place any longer." Petra, instead of walking out the door, walked up to Martha behind the desk where she was sitting, leaned down, and kissed her on the cheek.

I didn't do that, though. I waved to Martha and gave her a contrite little smile. She smiled warmly back, because that was Martha. Walking out the door with Petra behind me, I didn't notice the mayor until we were outside. He insisted on following me home. Well, first to Petra's and then home. He had no lights or sirens on though, because he didn't have any. But I thought I'd throw that in.

We arrived at Petra's, and I waited to drive off until she entered her house and flashed the porch lights at me. When I pulled into my driveway I waved to the mayor, but he waited until I walked inside the door and flashed my porch light at him before he drove off. That was kind of him, especially after my outburst in the council room. I'd have to give him credit for that. What I thought, though, was that Mayor Joe Stoddard was blaming himself for what happened. He was starting to have his doubts whether selling the historical society building was such a good idea or not.

It wasn't. And I was glad he felt bad. It was a historical building, for cryin' out loud! It needed to be preserved, not made into an indoor mall or something, which was the rumor circulating around town. The whole episode made me think about the building, how much I liked it, and how much I enjoyed working there. And it got me to thinking.

Still dwelling on the situation, I walked into the bedroom to change clothes, but I didn't get to dwell long because Aiden called. Aiden was my son—er, *our* son. It would take me a while to get used to thinking that way, now that Billy and I were married. After meeting Aiden in an unusual way and then briefly becoming his advocate, I started adoption procedures, much to his and my delight. The adoption wasn't final yet, the court appearance would be next month. Aiden couldn't wait for it to be final! We had both waited a long time for that to happen.

I pushed the speaker button on my phone, so I could take my shoes and clothes off while I talked to him.

"Hi, sweetie."

"Hi, Mommy! I miss you!"

"I miss you, too, Aiden."

"How did the council meeting go? Did you stop them from selling the building?"

Aiden had a fondness for the building, too, because that's where we first met. "No, I didn't, but the sale is stopped for now. Daddy or I will tell you about it when we see you."

"Oh. I could look it up on the internet, but not here, because Lily broke the monitor on the computer."

Lily was his second cousin and his best friend. And to say she was a wild child would be like saying a tyrannosaurus rex was kinda mean. Her parents—my cousin Kasey and her husband John—let her get away with anything and everything, and never reprimanded her. Aiden was a little wild when he visited her, but I decided not to make him behave when he was over there. It wouldn't be fair.

"You can't fix it?" I asked him. Aiden was a computer whiz. If anybody could fix it, he could.

"No, the screen is too broken. Can I talk to Daddy? I miss him, too."

"Sorry, Aiden, but Daddy had to work late tonight."

"Oh, is—" I heard him say something not into the phone. "Mommy, Lily just hit me with a ball trying to get me off the phone, so I better go. She might throw the monitor at me next! Bye! I love you!" I sure hoped he was kidding. Lily wasn't strong enough to throw a computer monitor, was she?

CHAPTER SIX

ALTHOUGH I WASN'T happy about the prospect of Lily throwing a computer monitor at Aiden, I was grateful she had distracted him from asking what his Daddy was doing. Aiden had an uncanny ability to deduce what was happening from the most insignificant details. And it would be better if Billy explained the situation to him. Billy was more tactful than I was. A girl has to know her limitations, you know?

After getting undressed and putting on my robe, I walked into the living room and sat on the couch. I loved my house. It was an adorable red gambrel—that kind of house that looks like a barn —painted bright red with white trim. One thing I loved about the house was how cozy it felt inside. There was a wood stove in the living room, and a breakfast bar separating the living room from the kitchen. It had two bedrooms and an office.

Unfortunately, Billy felt the house was too small for the three of us. He thought the house he had been fixing up would be perfect. It was on Hillside Terrace—the street with all the mansions on it—his house was elegant, but on the smaller side. Still, it wasn't my kind of place. I wished he could make do with my beloved little gambrel, but it's not where he wanted to live. He said he had something else in mind, but he hadn't showed it to me yet.

I stretched out my legs and picked up my book. The author referred to it as a reincarnational novel, and it was interesting. I wasn't sure whether or not I believed in reincarnation, but it was a good book just the same. Aiden and I, and Billy, too, were all big readers. After finishing two or three chapters, I lay my head back on the couch and started thinking about the historical society building again.

But I didn't get to think too long because Billy called. He said everything was going smoother than he thought, and he'd be home in an hour and a half, unless something unexpected occurred. But having been a cop's wife for less than a week, I had already learned that expecting the unexpected was part of the deal.

He didn't get home until after midnight, and I had fallen asleep on the couch. He thought I had waited up for him and he pulled me up off the couch, put his arms around me in a warm embrace, and kissed me. "Thanks for waiting up for me."

Lying to your not-quite-a-week new husband was not a good idea, so I confessed. But Billy, understanding as usual, said, "But you didn't go to bed," he said. "That proves you *meant* to wait up for me, and that's good enough for me."

Too tired to argue, I sank back down on the couch. "You're not mad at me?" I asked, thinking about my outburst at the meeting.

"I expected it! Why do you think I didn't sit with you?" He laughed. After drinking a glass of water, he sat beside me and put his arm around me. "Besides, it could have been worse. I don't know how, but it could have been."

I ignored his comment, but he was probably right. "So what happened? Any leads?"

He slowly moved his head from side to side without really shaking it. "Noooo." He drew it out to one long word.

"What does *that* mean? Who did everybody think did it?"

He looked at me and squinched up his face. I thought he was going to cry. "Almost everyone thinks Martha did it."

"Martha!" I clapped my hands and laughed. "You've got to be kidding. Come on, tell me the truth. Who does everyone think?"

Billy looked at me still frowning. "Martha."

"You're not kidding? Oh, no! How could they think that?" Without waiting for him to answer, I continued. "*You* don't think she did it, do you?"

"Of course not, Lorry." But he said it a little too crossly which made me wonder if he had his doubts. "She's like a mother to me. And a grandmother to Aiden."

That was all true. Martha, and her husband Hugo had "adopted" both Billy and I. And Aiden and I had stayed with them for several weeks in their bed and breakfast while our house was in escrow. That's why Aiden called Martha and Hugo *Grammy* and *Grampy*. "You don't sound very sure, Billy."

"I know Martha loves you, but I can't imagine her killing someone to save your job. I just can't see it."

"Of course she wouldn't do that. Martha is incapable of murder. You've seen her catch spiders in that plastic glass of hers and put them outside. She can't kill *anything*. Why would you even question it? Just because *everyone* thinks so? Billy, you've learned that lesson already."

"Yes, and after what happened to my father, I said I wouldn't let it happen to me."

"Need I remind you, Billy Madrigal, when I was accused of murder, you confessed to me that you realized your father was right."

His arm was still around me, and after I said that, he squeezed me to him and kissed me on the cheek. "That's one reason I love you, Lor. You're not afraid to tell me the truth. You tell me what I need to hear."

"Well, it's not like I have a choice, Billy. I just blurt that stuff out without thinking!"

He kissed me again. "Don't remind me!" He said it in a harsh tone, but he was kidding and smiled at me. "You know what? I miss Aiden."

This was our first night alone without Aiden since we had gotten married. You'd think he would say something *else*, but that wasn't my Billy. And I felt grateful for that. It made me feel more loved that he loved Aiden as much as I did. If that makes any sense. Well, it makes sense to me, and that's all that matters. Besides, Billy has no equal in that other department. Believe me, he has no equal. If you know what I mean.

CHAPTER SEVEN

AS WE ATE breakfast the next morning, we discussed the case again. "What made everyone think it was Martha? Not just because she likes me. That doesn't even make sense."

"Because she said she was in the bathroom, and no one saw her go in or out. Christa said she was in the bathroom and never saw Martha. Russell Tabor said he walked by and saw Christa coming out."

"Maybe they're in it together," I said, but it didn't sound right even to me.

"Ah, I don't think there was more than one person in on this. Besides, Christa voted for the sale. It makes sense the motive for this murder has to do with the sale, but I'm not totally convinced."

"Why not?"

"I don't know. It was a little too *convenient*."

"Maybe it was convenient because it was, you know, convenient to kill him right then. You haven't ruled anyone out yet, except you, me, the mayor, and Wichita. With everybody a suspect, it takes the heat off the real killer. I think it was clever."

"You could be right. Still, I'm not closing my mind to other possibilities."

I pushed back from the kitchen table and put my hands on my hips. "Are you trying to say *I* have a closed mind?" Pointing to myself, I added, "Moi?" I can't speak French, but I can ad-lib with the best of them.

"Well, um, I," Billy started, then straightening up, he looked at me and said, "No, Lorry, I'm not exactly saying that, but we both know it's true. Once you have your mind made up about somebody, not much can change it. Remember—" But he didn't get to finish because his phone rang.

"Sheriff Madrigal . . . Oh, yes, thanks. I'll be right there. Bye."

He stood up from the table, and while he rinsed his dishes and put them in the dishwasher, he said, "I forgot. My first interview starts right now."

"I thought you got everybody last night?"

"No, I just fingerprinted them, checked for GSR, and asked them a few basic questions. Everybody wanted to go home, and so did I. Anything that couldn't wait, I asked, but there were several more questions that didn't hurt to wait. It was better for everybody that way. Anyway, gotta leave, sweetie." He bent over to kiss me. "I love you, and I'll see you later." Before he reached the door, he turned around and said, "Remind me later to tell you the weird thing about the GSR." Then he walked to the front door and left, leaving me sitting alone in the kitchen thinking about my closed mind.

Well, he was right. How many times in the past few months had I been absolutely, positively sure that I knew who the murderer was only to be wrong? But it was also true that I ultimately came up with the real killer—sometimes almost too late. So I had a closed mind and a judgment problem and who knows what else. I was working through all that, right? So if I acknowledged I had the problem and was working on it, then I was on the right track, right? Judgmentals Anonymous. My name is Lorry Lockharte and I'm judgmental.

I let go of those confusing thoughts when the wall phone in the kitchen rang. "Hello! . . . Aiden! . . . No, sorry, you missed him. He already left for work. . . . I know, sweetie. I love you, too. . . . And I'm looking forward to seeing you. . . . Okay, love you, bye."

Jerri Kay Lincoln

What a great kid I had! What a great husband I had! What a lucky person I was! And this lucky person would be late for work if I dawdled any longer, so I got dressed, got ready, and left the house.

When I walked into the back of the historical society and past Petra's desk, she grumped a hello at me. "What's up with you?" I asked. "I thought you'd be celebrating."

"Lorry, *somebody* died last night. How can I celebrate that?"

"You seemed happy last night."

"I wasn't happy about that, I was happy because Mason was there, and I feel safe with Mason." Without turning around, she added, "You know, safe. Old French. Circa 1300. Meaning un-scathed, uninjured, free from danger."

Since I thought that was a weird thing to say, I dropped it. But thinking back on that comment, I should have known something was up. But I was too concerned with myself to notice—not that I could have changed anything. I don't think I could have. But it makes a person think.

After checking my email, I walked past Petra's desk again, not saying a word this time, and trudged up the stairs. Another computer was up there, attached to the scanner, and that was what I had been working on before the threat of imminent closure disrupted my work. Time to get back to it. Yes, it was possible Todd Fenton, the son, would still buy the building, but I didn't think anything would happen for a while. And although I had some thoughts on the subject, nothing had firmed itself up in my mind yet. Not that I had a firm mind to begin with—mine was more soggy and jiggly, but thorough. Still, nothing had come to mind. Nothing, you know, firm, anyway.

I heard the bell on the front door jingle, so I hurried down-stairs—with Bingo at my heels—so the visitors wouldn't disturb Petra. She was studying, after all. As the person began stepping in the door, I was delighted it was Martha—until I saw the look on her face. "Martha! What's the matter?"

She threw her arms up in the air and back down again to her sides. When I noticed there were tear stains on her cheeks, I immediately wrapped my arms around her in a hug. I didn't need to call Petra, because she heard the alarm in my voice and joined me in hugging Martha.

"Oh, dear, Lorry, how did you ever take it when they accused you of murder? Everybody looks at me like I'm a pariah!"

"You know how I took it, Martha?" I asked without letting up on my hug. "I took it because I had good friends like you and Petra who believed in me. And you know *we* believe in you."

"We know you didn't do it, Martha!" said Petra.

"How could you possibly kill someone, Martha, when you can't even kill a spider?"

That made her laugh, and she relaxed a little in our group hug.

CHAPTER EIGHT

AFTER WE CALMED Martha down, Petra walked her back to work. Petra and I had tried to convince her to take some time off while Billy solved the murder, but she'd have nothing of it. In her words, she "wouldn't let a bunch of short-sighted busy-bodies keep me from doing my job." That made Petra and I laugh, but we still tried to talk her out of returning to work. Although we couldn't, by the time Petra returned, I had already called Hugo to tell him what happened and to suggest maybe he could surprise her for lunch. Knowing Hugo, he would probably jump out of a cake with a sack lunch in his hand. That would surprise her for sure. I just hoped he had clothes on when he did it.

Petra was back at her desk studying as I walked by. The bell above the front door jingled as I started up the stairs, so with a grunt of frustration, I turned around and returned to the front. It was Christa Hawthorne. She was dressed head to toe in designer clothes, and she smelled like stale cigarettes. She wore a purple Chanel sweater with lavender embroidered hearts. And her Versace slacks fit her slim figure as tight as the sweater did. In her long, dark hair she wore a red ribbon with diamonds, yes, diamonds, sewn onto each end. And her purple Gucci high-heeled pant boots matched perfectly. Keep in mind, though, Christa owned a boutique. Dressing like that was required.

Since her boutique was on the other side of the Rutledge Koffee Korner Kafe, I had seen her plenty of times standing out front smoking. Aiden and I walked to the library on the corner several times a week. She was always polite and said hello, maybe even a "how are you" but never more than that. What was she doing here?

"Hello, Lorry!" she said, as she walked in as if we were the best of friends. She closed the door behind her and shook my hand.

"Hello, Christa," I said hesitantly.

"I wanted to offer my condolences."

I had no idea what she was talking about, but she looked contrite, so I said, "Thank you, but I don't know what you're talking about."

Christa put her hand on my shoulder, tilted her head, and smiled the kind of pitying smile like if a neighbor's cat just got run over and they didn't know it yet. "You know, with the sale of the historical society, you'll be losing your job." She took her hand off my shoulder and took a single step back. "I know you don't need the money, but I also know how important this job is to you."

She took a quick glance around as if wondering why it would be important to me. But her voice was so soothing it calmed me. "With the buyer dead, I thought the sale was on hold," I said.

"Only temporarily. I'm sure the son will carry through with the sale since that's what his father wanted—and of course he will inherit the business, so it's in his best interest. But I was talking more about Martha being the main suspect in the murder. When she loses her job as the town manager, then your job will most certainly be in jeopardy." She stuck out her hand again and patted me gently on the shoulder with a slight tilt of the head. "I'm so sorry, Lorry."

Her words were annoying, but she said them with such sincerity and compassion, it made me like her. Before I could utter even a thank you, she pushed up the sleeve of her sweater and looked at her Rolex watch.

"Oh! I've got to get back. Nice talking to you, Lorry. Stop by the shop sometime." Christa opened the door, but before she stepped out, she looked at me with big cow eyes. "Again, I'm sorry the way everything turned out for you." Then she disappeared out the door.

"Wow," I said. "She's so nice. I never realized that. I always thought she was a b—" I began to say, but Petra stopped me.

"Lorry, you know you can't say that in this genre."

"What?" I asked.

"Never mind," said Petra. "Ask Aiden. He'll know what I mean."

"All right, whatever. But I was going to add now that I know she's so nice, I might shop at her store. I always thought she only sold cheap knockoffs, but the clothes she was wearing were all *real*."

"You always judge people before you know their whole story. I would have thought you had learned that lesson by now."

"I guess I'm still learning," I said. "Are *you* worried, Petra? Even if they don't sell the historical building, if they fire Martha, the new person could close it down due to lack of interest, or something else they could easily come up with. Although I don't think Martha is in any danger of being fired, Christa is on the council, and maybe she knows something we don't."

"She probably does, Lorry, but you need to chill. You're too young to have a heart attack, but you're going in that direction. There are some things you can't stop from happening. No matter how much you don't want it to happen, you know it will and you can't do anything about it. Just let it go and deal with the consequences." She said it in a way that made me think she wasn't talking about the historical society at all.

Putting my hands on my hips, I stood beside her desk. "You're philosophical today. What's up with that?"

"I'm going back to studying." And she turned toward her computer, and all I saw was her petite back with the bright red blouse she wore.

Starting up the stairs again, I was once again stopped when I heard the bell on the front door jingle with another visitor. I hoped it would be someone as pleasant as Christa. But it wasn't.

CHAPTER NINE

KASEY BRANNIGAN WAS my cousin. We had never been close, though before the *event* happened, Billy, Aiden, and I would share activities and dinners with Kasey, her husband John, and her two children. Lily, the oldest, was Aiden's best friend, and Zandor, the infant named after a weather channel winter storm that never happened. But after Kasey was accused of murder, things became a little tense between us. It had been a while since then, though, and everything was almost back to normal. Almost being relative.

Today she wore what she wore every day she worked: a bright yellow waitress uniform with yellow tennis shoes to match. The uniform also matched the bright yellow part of the building that the Rutledge Koffee Korner Kafe occupied at the Rutledge Historical Building. That had happened years ago, and I still hated it. The historical building was a grand old building defaced by the yellow portion of the building that became the Kafe. Maybe someday someone could restore the building to her former glory. I could only wish.

"Hi, Lorry! I thought I'd stop by and say hello since once again you're the talk of the town."

"Oh?" was all I said. With Kasey, squeezing in one or two words at a time was all you're *allowed*.

"Yeah! Another murder in Rutledge! Whoever thought so many people could get murdered in a town this small. Well, it's grown, but, you know, it's still small. And you haven't even been back here a year yet and look how many people have been murdered!" She leaned forward as if to tell me a secret, but spoke in her normal voice. "And people are saying maybe you've jinxed the town—you know, with all the people who've been killed since *you've* returned. They're wondering who will be next."

Putting my hands on my hips and narrowing my eyes at her, I asked, "Kasey, exactly *who* has been saying that maybe I've jinxed the town?"

Mimicking my actions, she put her hands on her hips and narrowed her eyes. "That would be little ole me. You know, Cruella DeVille."

I had called Kasey Cruella DeVille—after the villain who stole the Dalmatians—since first grade when she stole my first boyfriend, Conrad Hayes. And no, he wasn't really my boyfriend, and no, she didn't really steal him, but it felt that way, and to a first-grader it felt really bad. I had never called her Cruella DeVille to her face and had no idea she even knew I called her that, but after the murder episode, a lot of truth came out into the world.

She and her husband John were still trying to repair the damage the whole episode caused their marriage. She and I were trying, too. But apparently, Kasey and I weren't doing a very good job. Kasey still resented me for calling her that and still blamed me for it. And I couldn't blame her since she had known about it all these years but only mentioned it at her time of crisis.

So I took my hands off my hips, fastened a frown on my face, and said, "You're still holding that against me?"

Kasey *didn't* take her hands off her hips. "You called me that for, let's see, how many years? And it happened when we were, what? Six years old? And I didn't steal him, anyway! So if I hold that against you for even half the time you called me that, then I would say I still have a decade or so to go."

"All right, Kasey, all right." I wasn't going to say *I'm sorry*, so I tried to get back to the subject at hand. Kasey did have a knack for finding out information, and that information could be useful. "So what else are they saying?"

"Well, almost no one thinks Martha did it, despite the town council thinking so. And that is mostly Douglas Gates and that big-mouth Anthony Petrelli. He talks more than I do! He's spreading it all over town that Martha killed that guy Fenton trying to protect your job—which makes no sense since you don't need the money."

Kasey said it matter-of-factly with no edge to her voice. She could have resented me because of the money I inherited, but I didn't think she did. Being a member of the extended family, she knew what I had to put up with from my mother. No amount of money could repay me for that. Can I call it abuse? I never have, but I think it fits.

"Anyway, Lorry, I thought I'd come over and share the rumors with you. I figured you'd be interested."

"And you wouldn't have told me you were the one who started them if I hadn't asked?"

She laughed, but it wasn't the funny kind of laugh. "Of course I would have told you! What fun would it be if I kept it to myself?" Then she turned around, opened the door and sashayed through it, skipping back to the cafe after closing the door behind her.

CHAPTER TEN

AS I WATCHED Kasey disappear, I shook my head. It looked like she'd never let me forget that I called her Cruella DeVille for so many years. And maybe that is as it should be. When she brought it up, I could have mentioned all the times—since I moved back—she had gotten me in trouble by shooting off her big mouth telling everybody's brother my business. In all honesty, though, I knew better than to tell her those items, anyway, so I created my own problems with that. It was my own fault for opening *my* big mouth.

From the other room, I heard Petra say, "Who's coming in next? The Easter Bunny?"

"It's a little early for him," I answered.

Since I had been so unsuccessful at getting up the stairs so far, I checked my email again before attempting the climb. There was nothing of import there, some funny forwards from friends along with some animal pictures. The most interesting email was an official invite from Mason—at least that's what he called it—for a chess match. He said if I wasn't interested, maybe Aiden would be. Mason had taught Aiden how to play chess, and Aiden had caught on quickly but wasn't much interested. He preferred board games with a little more variety to them. His favorite right now was called Stone Age.

When I finished declining Mason's offer, I stood up to try the stairs again, but someone opened the door before I took even one step.

"Is it the Easter Bunny?" asked Petra.

"I'd make a sound like a rabbit, but I don't know what that would be," said Billy. "Ribbit, ribbit? No, I think that's a frog." He put his arms around me and gave me a tight squeeze and a kiss. "How's my bride on this fine morning?"

"Better, now that you're here."

He cocked his head and looked at me. "Everything all right?"

"Yes, fine, but do you know what they're saying about Martha?"

Billy frowned and nodded. "Yes, I told you yesterday what they thought, and the few interviews I've had this morning all say the same thing. If it wasn't you, then it has to be her."

"What can we do, Billy? Martha isn't as tough as I am, and I'm not sure she can take it. I'm worried about her."

"Well, I still have several more interviews to go, but if they continue with the tack they're taking, it will be a long night."

"Billy, wait, before you go, tell me the weird thing about the gunshot residue."

"Oh, yeah. It's really weird." He glanced around and saw no one in the gift shop. "Anyone in the back?"

"No, just Petra."

"I'm not anyone?" yelled Petra from the office behind mine.

"Of course you're anyone, Petra. Just not for the current subject. You don't count," I said.

Billy walked the few steps to her office, kissed her on the head like he always did, and said, "You're always someone to me, Petra." They were close. And that was a good thing because of her no-account father. She needed someone like Billy in her life.

When he returned, he checked his watch, took me by the shoulders, and looked into my eyes. "Listen, Lorry, the murder is not what I came here to talk to you about. I don't have that much time before the next interview starts. And I wanted to tell you that I bought a house today."

Not knowing what to say, I remained silent. He bought a house for us to live in and didn't let me see it first? That didn't sound right. So instead of jumping in with both feet and winding up with said feet dangling from my mouth, I decided to wait and see what he said.

"You're not going to yell at me?" he asked, with a tentative smile on his face.

"I'm listening," I said, trying to keep the edge out of my voice.

"It's a house I've been thinking about—I may have even mentioned it to you already—but something happened this morning. I would have waited and brought you and Aiden out to see it, except someone else put a bid on it, so I had to act right away or lose it." He squeezed my shoulders. "If you don't like it, I'll put it back on the market right away, and we can look for something else. Is that okay?"

"That sounds fine to me. And fair. When do Aiden and I get to see it?"

"This afternoon would be perfect if I can finish the interviews in time, and I'm pretty sure I can. How 'bout that?"

"We'll be ready!" I told him.

"Gotta run. Bye, sweetie." He kissed me on the lips and opened the door. "Bye, Petra! Ribbit! Ribbit!" Then he chuckled and stepped out the door.

"What was that about?" asked Petra.

"You mean the ribbit thing or the house thing?"

"The house. I don't care about the ribbit." She cleared her throat and continued, "Etymology: ribbit. Onomatopoeic. Vocal sound made by a frog or toad. Okay, now tell me about the house."

"Billy bought a house, and hopefully he'll bring me and Aiden out to see it today. If we don't like it, he'll sell it and we'll pick out something else together."

"Are you mad?"

"Why should I be?"

"Because you're married now, and he did it without talking to you about it first."

"He explained it all, and besides, I'm more mellow now."

"Yeah, right," said Petra. "And no longer judgmental, either. Did he say anything about the case?"

"Only that it might be a long night. I'm not sure what that means, but it doesn't sound good for Martha."

"Maybe this would be a good time for Martha and Hugo to go on vacation until all this blows over."

"She can't," I said.

"Why not?"

"Because even though you and I know she didn't do it, technically, she's still a suspect and isn't supposed to leave town."

I walked through Petra's office on my way back up the stairs. She shook her head as she typed into her computer and said, "What a crazy mixed-up world this is, huh? The sweetest, most compassionate person in the universe is suspected of killing someone. What next?"

CHAPTER ELEVEN

SINCE I HAD already started up the stairs numerous times unsuccessfully, this time I tried something different. I slipped off my three-inch heels and ran up the stairs. Two steps from the top, I heard the jingling of the front door opening, and I groaned. Petra must have heard me, because she said, "No worries, Lorry. I'll get this one."

Then I heard, "Oh, hi, Sam. Lorry's upstairs."

"Hi, Petra! Thanks!"

Sam was my old friend from high school who had moved away to college but had recently moved back with her family. Her son and Aiden were in the same class.

Standing at the top of the stairs, I smiled as she climbed up. "Hey, Sam!" It was always good to see Sam.

She stopped on the stairs. "Hey, Lorry. I was in the neighborhood. Do you have time for some coffee?" I must have frowned at the thought, because she said, "Oh? Cousin troubles again?" Then she shrugged and squeezed her lips together in an apologetic smile. "Sorry I don't have time to go anywhere else. I have to pick up Willow and take her for a doctor's appointment."

I forgot my discomfort for a moment. "Is she okay?"

Sam knocked on the sidewall of the staircase and said, "Oh, she's fine, kenahora. It's a routine appointment."

Since I began hanging around with Sam again, I was starting to pick up on the Yiddish words with which she liberally doused her speech. "Kenahora. I thought that was the Jewish equivalent of 'knock on wood.' But you knocked on the wall, anyway."

"Doesn't hurt to cover all your bases! So, do you want to go despite the location?"

"Sure. It's been an interesting morning—and Kasey was part of the reason. What the hey. Let's go." I slipped on my shoes, walked down the stairs, told Bingo to stay under my desk, followed Sam out the door, and braced myself for another clash with Kasey.

There wasn't any. There were three other tables with people, and they all had coffee and croissants in front of them. Their water glasses were all full. Kasey was talking on the phone, but brought it over to our table to take our order. She talked non stop into the phone but managed to write down our order. I splurged. I got a croissant, too. It took too much will power to say no when I could see how good they looked.

"How's married life?" Sam asked, after Kasey delivered our order still talking on the phone.

"It hasn't even been a week yet!" Smiling, I shook my head. "What a change from Eddie! Billy is an absolute dream. I don't know how I got so lucky."

"You deserved to get lucky, Lorry."

I nodded. "I did, didn't I?" And we both laughed.

We had our backs to the table of people next to us, but could hear every word of their conversation. And when my eyes raised at mention of "the town manager," Sam kept quiet.

"Yeah," the man said. "They're going to oust the current town manager, and the mayor is going to appoint someone new. Maybe even promote Russ Tabor, the town clerk, to manager."

"I don't believe it," said the woman sitting beside him. "Martha does a great job."

"I've got it on good authority that it's true," the man countered.

"Whose authority? Russ's? That's just wishful thinking."

"No, not Russ. Anthony Petrelli, who's on the High Council, told me."

"You mean Anthony 'true or true?' Petrelli?" The two women and the man at the table laughed.

That was one of Petrelli's favorite lines. I found that out when I bought my previous car—a Taurus—from him last year.

"What he said was, "Listen, a high council can't have someone representing the town if they're accused of murder. Am I right or am I right?"

They all laughed again at Petrelli's *second* favorite line. And I was about to open my mouth and shut down the whole conversation, but luckily—I think—Sam put her hand on my arm to quiet me.

The man slurped up the last of his coffee and stood up. "Well, we better get back to work, or we'll be ousted."

The three of them stood and walked out the door, leaving me silent but seething. After taking a sip of coffee, I chomped down on the croissant.

"So it's not true then—about Martha?" Sam leaned forward and whispered.

"You've met Martha," I said. "Have you ever met a nicer, more compassionate person? Of course she didn't do it. But this is how my morning's been going. I've had to listen to all this garbage."

"Is the council really going to oust her, though?"

"The whole council, except the mayor, is still under suspicion. The mayor was talking to Billy, Wichita, and me. Billy gave them a partial interview last night and is giving more complete ones today. *Everyone* is still a suspect at this point."

Sam looked at her watch and stood up. "I need to take off, Lorry." She tilted her head and smiled sadly at me. "Sorry you have to go through this. At least you have Billy!"

I nodded. "Thank goodness for Billy!"

Sam nodded, left money on the table, hugged me, picked up what was left of her coffee, and hurried out the door. I took the last bite of my croissant, another sip of coffee, put my money next to Sam's, stood up, waved to Kasey—who wasn't watching

—and returned to the historical society. I stayed long enough to tell Petra that I was leaving again and sidled out the back door.

CHAPTER TWELVE

ANTHONY PETRELLI'S CAR lot was two blocks across and three blocks long. After walking down the alley toward Bridge Street, I turned right and walked down two more blocks. It was on the corner of Bridge Street and Church Street—Church Street so named because that's where the church was. Duh.

I had my strategy all planned before I set foot on the lot. If Anthony suspected me of trying to pump information—or evidence—out of him, he would clam up like a, well, like a clam. The best tactic for finding anything out from him was to shut up. It sounds counterintuitive, but Anthony was a talker and liked to talk. So I planned to let him.

First part of the plan, though, was to figure out what kind of car I wanted to buy. Although I didn't really want to buy a new car since the car I had was almost new and I loved it, I needed a reason to be on the lot looking. So I decided on a Cadillac. That would get his attention.

He called his lot Motors and Masterpieces. The *motors* were the regular cars, both used and new, and the *masterpieces* were some pristine old classics. Yes, he had 65 Mustangs and 57 T-birds, but his prized possessions were a 1928 Model A and a 1950 Bentley.

For those of you who don't know, a Bentley is like a Rolls Royce, but reserved for those with more *discerning* taste. At least that's what Aiden says. Neither Billy nor I had any interest in cars, but Aiden had somehow become an aficionado. Don't hold that against him, though. Aiden is an expert in a lot of different areas, because he reads like a fish. Where did I ever come up with that simile? I have no idea, but as mixed-up as it sounds, it fits perfectly. He's also extremely competent on the computer, but his first love is books.

When I walked onto the lot, I had my fingers crossed that Anthony himself and not one of his salesmen would approach me. I knew he still did sales on his own, because when I bought my used Taurus here less than a year ago, he sold it to me. That car was long gone now, though, having met a bad, um, end.

Anthony's prices were good, and for a used car lot, it had a reputation of being honest. Some said that was because of the car lot's proximity to the church, but I didn't really know. Can someone be honest and still be a killer? Could I come right out and ask him if he killed that man? Probably not a good tactic. Wrapped up as I was in searching for the Cadillac section and in my thoughts, it surprised me when Anthony came out of nowhere.

"What are you doing here snooping through my car lot?" He said with his hands on his hips. "You have no business here. True or true?" Anthony said that a lot. You'll probably hear it again before the conversation ends.

"I'm looking for a car," I said, without looking at him. I continued toward the rows of Cadillacs I had spotted.

"You just got a car! And not from me!" He said, following me.

"If you know that much, then you know I am not the one who decided or bought it. Someone did it for me, and I left all the details up to him."

"Who lets someone else choose and buy a new car for them?" He said with disdain.

I turned toward him for the first time now, allowed him to catch up and spoke right into his face. I had to bend down. He was short. "The kind of person who is wrongly accused of murder and has other thoughts in her head than what kind of car to buy!" Turning back toward the Cadillacs, I walked toward them, still talking. "Although I'm keeping that car, I'm thinking I would like a Cadillac as well. You know, something special for when we go out."

It was like he had just noticed where we were headed. And now his business sense took over. "Oh!" He quickened his step to catch up to me. Anthony Petrelli was short, built like a spark plug, had jet black hair and dark eyes. He had a bad haircut. "What kind of Cadillac were you looking for?"

Now we were headed in the right direction. I don't mean toward the Cadillacs; I mean conversationally. And now to set him up for a talk-fest. "Something fancy. Billy and I went with Hugo and Martha to Sedona before we got married. Their car was comfortable and beautiful. Something like theirs."

His hands returned to his hips. "Martha! What is it with you and her? Kissing cousins or something? She's a murderer! I know it's her!"

He would have gone on talking, but I interrupted him. If he suspected he was doing what I wanted him to do, he would have shut up in an instant. "Anthony, fine. Whatever. Just show me a car like hers. I liked it a lot. It was beautiful and very comfortable to ride in." If I encouraged him at all, he would suspect what he *should* suspect—that I was baiting him.

We walked toward another car, and he continued talking the whole time. "It *was* her, and I think you know it! Everyone on the council knows it! It's not just me suspecting her blindly! I'm not an idiot! Another council member saw Christa coming out of the bathroom. No one saw Martha, and that's where she said she was. And you know what that equals? *She* did it! Am I right or am I right?"

I ignored his stupid question and said, "I didn't realize Russ Tabor was on the council," as I opened the door of the car and slid my fat butt inside.

"He may not exactly be on the council, but he's on the same side, at least. Don't you get it, Lorry? She has no alibi! It has to be her!"

Who knew that he knew my name? I guess the whole town knew my name after my crazy outburst at the council meeting the other night. "So I guess the whole council agrees with you?" Before he could answer, I added, "Is this car top of the line? Because I want a top of the line car," to make sure he didn't think I was pumping him for information, which was exactly what I was doing.

"Of course it's top of the line! You're a Lockharte, right? True or true!" He shook his head and started in again. "What I don't understand is why Martha would try to save your job when you don't even *need* a job. It makes no sense. Still, she doesn't have an alibi." Yawning, he looked around the lot and looked distracted. And I needed him to keep talking.

"Anthony, can I take it for a spin?" I didn't want to, but anything to keep him talking.

He reached into his pocket and pulled out a dozen keys, each one carefully labeled. Luckily, he had this car's key with him. If he had to go back into the office to retrieve it, he might forget what he was ranting on and on about. He walked around the car, slid in beside me, handed me the key, and I started it up. It sounded like an expensive car—almost silent. Maybe I really would get a Cadillac. Although I had been pretending, it was sounding more and more like a good idea.

Anthony pointed the way out of the lot, and although he told me to turn right on School Street, where the high school was, I drove straight across the bridge toward Coyote Moon. As I've already mentioned, Coyote Moon used to be known as West Rutledge. And where I am now, Rutledge, used to be known as East Rutledge. When they built the Coyote Moon Casino, West Rutledge changed its name to match the casino, so East Rutledge changed its name to plain ole Rutledge.

Anthony frowned when he saw where I was going, but said nothing. Well, that's not exactly true. He kept droning on and on about Martha and the murder—which was exactly what I wanted him to do. I interrupted periodically to prove to him that I wasn't interested. It was all part of my plan, which—patting myself on the back here—was working quite well.

"And in these days, if you don't have an alibi, you're pretty much dead meat."

"Does everyone else have an alibi?" I asked innocently.

"The mayor was talking to you, the sheriff, and Wichita. You know that already."

"Does this car have that cool thing where you can connect your cell phone to it, so you can do hands-free talking?" More and more counties in Arizona were outlawing driving while talking.

"Of course it does. All new cars do—at least all the ones that I sell."

"Yes, I know the mayor has an alibi. What about the other council members? There were several other people there who might have had motives. How do I move the seat forward?" Although it didn't need to move forward, I wanted him to forget I had asked about the murder.

He directed me to the button and then continued. "Christa and Russ accounted for. Mayor accounted for. Elizabeth and Paul Gallagher were—I don't know where they were! They had alibis, though, and so did everyone else! What are you asking me those questions for? I thought you wanted to buy a car?" His face was getting a little red around the edges.

Ah oh. I figured I'd better get in the most important question before he went ballistic or something. We stopped at a stop sign, and I looked directly at him. "And what was your alibi, Anthony? Off with one of your little tarts, I expect?" Don't ask me where I came up with that one. It popped into my head. I'm not even going to claim it.

"Tarts! Tarts!" he exploded. And his face that was red before now looked like an overripe tomato ready to burst. "I don't have any tarts! I'm happily married!" He waved his left hand in front of my face and with his other hand pointed to his wedding ring. It was a plain gold band. He opened the door of the car like he was going to get out, but must have realized it was his car, so he closed it again. Crossing his arms across his chest, he said, "Turn this car around now!"

I turned it around, silently smiling to myself, but playing my part to the end. Then I asked, "Does it come with satellite radio?"

We had just crossed the bridge back into Rutledge and were still three blocks from the car lot. He ignored my question and shouted, "Pull over and get out of my car! We're done here!"

CHAPTER THIRTEEN

ANTHONY DROVE AWAY with a start, leaving behind exhaust and dirt flying through the air toward me. I didn't realize Cadillacs had that much pickup. Maybe I *would* consider getting one.

As I walked past High Street on my way toward the alley that led to the back of the historical society, I thought about how my smart alecky ways had messed up my questioning. I never got an answer out of him about an alibi. Tarts? Wherever did I come up with that? I swear, sometimes words come out of my mouth, and I don't even know where they come from. Tarts. Who knows?

Maybe I did get some valuable information out of him, though. Everyone on the council thought Martha did it, which had to mean one of them did it. I'm not discounting the son, though. His whereabouts during the murder were still unknown. Maybe the murder had nothing to do with the sale at all. Maybe it was a plain old family squabble. I was painfully aware of those. And what about how red Anthony's face got when I mentioned tarts? Did that mean he was unfaithful to his wife or that he was incensed I would ask such a thing because he wasn't that kind of guy? Who could tell?

I was ready to turn down the alley back to the historical society when I realized the Rutledge Super Market was right across the street. Not that I didn't know it was there, but it was who was *in it* that made me think again. Brent Lindsay, the owner and a member of the council. So right there and then, I crossed the street, looking both ways and ignoring the crosswalks on either end of the block. How daring of me! How adventurous! Okay, okay, it's neither one, but until I climb Mount Everest, this is as adventurous and daring as I get.

Rutledge Super Market hasn't always been super. When it first started, it was a small store on the corner of Bridge and School Street. Although High Street and School Street were the same street, they were on either side of Bridge Street. Now the market stretched down School Street for two blocks and across Bridge Street for two blocks. It was almost—you know—super.

The door opened when I stepped on the mat in front of it, inviting me into the bright interior. The most notable characteristic about the Rutledge Super Market were the big "R's" on the floor. At the beginning and end of each aisle, plus if the aisle split in the middle, there was a big yellow R in the center of an orange circle. And orange lines connected all the R's to each other. So it was almost like following the yellow brick road as you shopped, except, you know, it was orange.

As I stood by the shopping carts pondering on whether I wanted to just go see Brent Lindsay or if I wanted to pretend I was shopping and "accidentally" run into him, someone tapped me on the shoulder. Looking up, it surprised me to see Elizabeth Conroy standing in front of me.

"Hello, Lorry."

"Hello, Elizabeth." I was about to ask what she was doing there until I realized that would be redundant. "How are you?" That was innocent enough.

"Fine, thank you."

"Um, I'm fine, too," I stammered. "Where were you when that guy was killed?"

She laughed. "You get right to the point, don't you? I was reading the bulletins at the front of the building."

"So who do you think did it? Are you one of the not-so-silent majority who thinks Martha did it?"

Elizabeth was tall and thin, her dark hair starting to gray, and she was taller than me. Looking pensive, she nodded her head. "Lorry, I like to think of myself as independent, not part of any majority, but," she shrugged her shoulders, "sometimes the majority is right. Are they in this case? I don't know."

"You've known Martha a long time, Elizabeth. Do you honestly think she's capable of such a thing? And the whole rumor that she did it to save my job is ridiculous, don't you think, considering I could buy the whole town if I wanted to."

"Lorry, sometimes what's good for the majority is often the right thing to do, even if it's not the nice thing to do."

"You mean it might be more expedient to blame Martha whether she did it or not?"

"That's not exactly what I said, Lorry."

Although I had been out of high school for fifteen years, this woman still made me feel like I was back there. She had the kind of authoritarian bearing that demanded respect. So I waited for her to continue.

"You think Martha didn't have a motive, don't you? But she didn't want that sale to go through any more than you do, and I don't think it had anything to do with you. So keeping that in mind, can you be certain Martha didn't do it?" Elizabeth asked, tilting her head toward me like Bingo sometimes did.

As I was about to open my mouth and say how certain I was of Martha's innocence, I began to wonder. Martha didn't want the sale to go through and it had nothing to do with me? That was news. Did she have a motive? Somewhere in all that wondering, my mouth must have opened, because now I closed it without saying a word.

"See?" she said. "Billy hasn't declared anyone innocent, yet, right Lorry? The murderer could be any one of us. Including Martha."

I didn't like where the conversation had taken us, so I straightened up and spoke up. I was an adult now, and she was no longer my principal. "Then that includes you, too, Elizabeth, right?"

She smiled at me as she walked away. "Yes, Lorry, that includes me."

CHAPTER FOURTEEN

BY THIS TIME, I didn't have time to visit with Brent Lindsay, so I hurried back to the office to find Bingo curled up in my office chair. "How did he get up here?" I asked Petra.

"He kept whining for you, so I lifted him up, and he settled right down."

"My baby missed me." I picked him up and hugged him.

"Oh, please. Spare me the hyperbole. Latin, early fifteenth century. Obvious exaggeration in rhetoric."

I stomped into her office with my hands on my hips. "If he didn't miss me, then why was he crying?" I demanded.

"How should I know? Maybe he was hungry, and you left some crumbs on the seat of your chair."

At that moment Bingo yipped, so it made it easy for me to ignore Petra's soft laughter. Turning, I stomped down the hallway with Bingo at my heels. Trudging up the stairs, I sat down in front of the computer, flipped it on, flipped the scanner on, and thought about my morning. How sad that sweet innocent Martha was having to go through this. Although there wasn't much I could do about it, I hoped Billy could somehow stop the harassment.

I hadn't got much scanning done before I heard Aiden at the back door—not that the scanning mattered. If the building sold, all the scanning I had done would be for naught. Aiden ran in.

Bingo ran down the stairs to meet him, and after a brief huggy-kissy session, Aiden ran upstairs and threw his arms around me.

"Mommy! Mommy! I missed you so much!"

"Not as much as I missed you!" I kissed him on the cheek. "How was school?"

"Great as usual. I found out about the murder—looked it up on the internet. It was at the council meeting you were at, right? The guy who was going to buy this building."

"Yep, yep, and yep," I said.

"Tell me more!"

"You can ask your father when you see him. It's not my place."

Aiden gave me his sad face, but I shook my head. "You have to wait, kiddo." He stuck his lip out for effect—he had learned that from me, I'm sorry to say—but I shook my head again. "I have good news for you! Daddy is going to take us to see the new house he bought!"

"Really? A new house?" He stopped, narrowed his eyes, tilted his head, and looked at me. "Why would he buy a house without the rest of his family seeing it first?" Aiden had a righteous sense of propriety. He had probably gotten that from me, too. And I wasn't sure if that was good or bad.

"Yes, I know, I know. But he said it was a rush deal, and he had to do it or lose it. And he said if we didn't like it, he would sell it, and we would buy something else."

"All right," said Aiden, taking his time between words. Then, already over it, he added, "When's Daddy coming? At closing time?"

"No, he said if the interviews went as planned, he might get here early. He mentioned having to work tonight, though."

"Do sheriff's families always have to suffer with their loved one working late?"

That made me laugh. "Aiden, honey, it would be worse if we lived in a big city. Daddy doesn't have to work late that often. We should feel grateful for when he's home with us."

Rocky, the cat who lived at the Rutledge Historical Society, jumped down from the high shelf he was on, and rubbed against Aiden's legs. Aiden petted him, and Bingo sniffed his butt.

I turned back to the scanning, but didn't have time to scan even one more document, because I heard Billy come in through the back door. He called out, "Any chance my new bride and my boy are here waiting for me?"

"Careful going down the stairs, Aiden!"

My words were too late, because he had already reached the bottom and was in Billy's arms. I could hear him squeal as Billy swung him around. Bingo barked at his feet.

"Lor? You ready? I want you both to have enough time to see all the house and grounds. And I have to get back here before too late. Let's go!"

Hurrying down the stairs, which wasn't all that fast because of my three-inch heels, I held on to the handrail. When I arrived at the bottom of the stairs, Billy threw his arms around me, kissing and hugging me. "Let's go, gorgeous."

"Petra, I'm leaving early today. Hope you don't mind."

"You've barely been here at all today, so what's the dif?"

I ignored her comment and followed Billy, Aiden, and Bingo out the back door. We all climbed into Billy's truck, none of us knowing where we were going except Billy. Aiden asked. "Daddy? Where are we going?"

"You'll find out soon enough, kiddo!" Billy started the truck and pulled out of the alley onto Bridge Street. Then he made an immediate left onto High Street.

"Did you forget something at the society?" I asked. I knew the house couldn't be on End Street and or on River Road, which apart from its cool name was a bunch of run down businesses that should have been run out of town a long time ago. Now that I thought about it, though, the only businesses that remained on River Road were a couple of junk yards. The auto parts store had cleaned up and moved to Commercial Street next to the tire store.

"Nope," he said.

I'd always considered that the historical society was at the end of High Street. It wasn't exactly a dead end, but as close as you could get without really being one. There was an empty lot on the other side of the society, and just past that was what once may have been a corner, but wasn't any longer. There was a big orange and white traffic barricade across the makeshift intersection. On each side of the barricade was just enough room for a car—or truck—to pass through. On the other side of it, after miles of dirt roads, were a handful of residences, though most of them were ranches. Billy passed through the barricade and continued down the rutted dirt road.

CHAPTER FIFTEEN

"WHERE ARE WE going, Daddy?" asked Aiden, with a hint of impatience in his voice. "There's nothing out here but ranches. I thought we were going to see the new house you bought."

"Wait and see," said Billy.

A couple of miles of rough washboard road later, I read a sign on the right side as we bounced by. It said *Private Road. Caution. Travel at your own risk. This surface is not regularly maintained.*

"Billy, are you sure about this?" I asked.

"No worries, hon. I've driven this road in all kinds of weather. We'll be safe."

"Yes, but assuming that Aiden and I like the house, can *I* drive this road in my Rav4?" My car was almost brand new, and I didn't want to get a different car. I loved my Rav4.

"It's got all-wheel drive, doesn't it?" asked Billy.

"Yup."

"You'll be fine. Don't worry so much."

Just then the truck hit a deep hole in the road sending the three of us into the air as far as the seat belts allowed. Bingo, formerly in the back seat with Aiden, ended up in the front seat with Billy and me. "Famous last words, eh, Billy?" This road gave a new meaning to "keeping you at the edge of your seats." We were there—literally.

"Sorry. I usually avoid that thing, but was too excited about both of you seeing the house."

Several miles and potholes later, with a few ranches in our rearview mirror, Billy turned left onto another dirt road. This road had a high fence to the left of it, and inside the fence was a horse grazing beside a tree-size juniper bush. At least, tree-size by Arizona standards.

"Are we almost there?" I asked.

"It's a ranch, Mom!" said Aiden, who was leaning forward and straining against his seat belt.

"Is it a ranch, Billy? Is the house you bought—*a ranch*?"

He looked at me, smiled, and squeezed my leg. To Aiden, he said, "What do you think, little pard?"

"I love it, Daddy! I love it!"

"You haven't even seen it yet, kiddo," Billy said.

"Yeah, but it's a *ranch*!" said Aiden. "And it's got *horses*!"

Billy squeezed my leg again. "What do you think, Lor?"

"Looks cool, but as you say, I haven't seen it yet."

As we approached, I looked over the property and saw more horse enclosures, a large rambling ranch house, a big barn, and some other kind of building. There were no neighbors anywhere around it. In a distant grassy area, on the other side of a fence, I saw some grazing cows.

"Aiden, look! There are cows over there!" I said.

"That's state land leased to ranchers for their cattle. And there is a gate, so we can ride over there," said Billy.

"What do the horses think of the cows?" I asked.

Billy smiled. "Some horses are okay with them, some aren't. My horse doesn't mind 'em at all."

"What about *my* horse, Daddy?"

"You don't have a horse yet, little pard!"

As we pulled under the signpost reminiscent of ranches in the old west, I noticed there were three roads going into the property. The right one went behind the house, the middle one went toward the house, and the left one went in between a big horse enclosure and then another enclosure with a high fence. It looked like it led to the barn.

Billy took the middle path and pulled up in front of the large double car garage. Most of the house was to the left of it with a small portion to the right. "You ready to see the inside?"

"Yeah!" said Aiden and was out of the car in a flash.

I looked around and took my time getting out, wondering if I could call this sprawling place *home*. Aiden was jumping up and down, and Billy picked him up and swirled him around, so I started walking toward the smaller portion of the house.

"Not that way, Lor, over here." He motioned me to follow him and Aiden who was now holding his hand. "That's the apartment. I'll show it to you later. Let's see the house first—see if you like it.

"Can Bingo come in the house with us?"

"He's family, isn't he? Of course!" Billy passed the first door—that appeared to lead inside the garage—and walked over to a double-doored entry. He used a key to open one of the doors. The three of us stepped inside.

Despite the late hour, the many windows let plenty of light inside to make it bright. The first thing I noticed besides the abundance of light was straight ahead—a wood-burning stove. It was bigger than the one in our little gambrel house, but it was a welcome sight. It also had one of those transparent fronts so I could watch the flames dance, which was one of my favorite activities on a cold winter's evening. And yes, there are cold evenings in the winter in Arizona. It sometimes even snowed!

I followed Billy and Aiden straight ahead into a living room full of gorgeous furniture. "Billy, when are they going to remove their furniture?"

"They only want one piece that I will have to get movers to pick up and send to them. The rest is ours—you know, if you want it. If not, we can get new furniture."

I *loved* the furniture. It had that lived-in, comfortable look that new furniture didn't have. New furniture often had that "stay-off-me, I'm new" look. I loved this furniture—the furniture in *our* new home.

CHAPTER SIXTEEN

"YOU READY TO see the rest of the house?" Billy asked. When I didn't say anything, he got a dubious look on his face. "You haven't seen it all yet. Do you hate it already?"

"Billy," I murmured, "I love it!" I threw my arms around him and gave him a big hug.

Aiden jumped in to join us and said, "I love it, too, Daddy!"

Billy's dubious look turned into the purest expression of joy that I had ever seen. "I'm so glad. I've loved this place for so long, and when it came up suddenly for sale, I knew I had to snag it. I'm so happy you both love it." A couple of tears escaped his eyes, but he blinked them away. I hoped that Aiden saw that. Real men can cry. And Billy was a real man.

"Here, Lor, sit down here. I want you to see something."

Sitting on the proffered love seat, I moved my hand along the fabric. "It's very comfortable. I love the suede."

"You ain't seen nuthin' yet, sister!" Billy leaned down to the side of the love seat and pushed a button.

"Oh!" I said when the love seat turned into a recliner on my side of the center console, which still had a remote control in it. "I didn't expect that! Very cool!"

Billy lowered the seat back down and helped me up from the spot that I would have liked to have stayed in.

"Me, too, Daddy! Me, too!" Aiden said.

"Okay, get in!" Billy waited until Aiden had climbed all the way into the chair on the other side of the console. "Here we go! Take off!"

"Whee!" said Aiden.

As I watched the two of them, I marveled at how easy Billy was with Aiden. He was in a hurry—I knew he had to get back to town, and he still took the time to give Aiden a ride without complaining. What a lucky person I was to have a guy like Billy.

"Okay, come on, kiddo. We have to look at the rest of the house." He helped Aiden out of the chair and looked at his watch. "And I want you to see the barn, too."

As much as I wanted to see *our new home*, I really wanted to process what I had found out this afternoon. So while Billy walked down the hallway showing off the house to the bouncing Aiden beside him, I settled into the love seat, pushed the button and let it recline all the way back. Aiden was enthusiastic enough for both of us.

After closing my eyes, I first went over my conversation with Anthony Petrelli. He had gone on and on that Martha did it and saying that the other council members thought she did, too. He also thought everyone had an alibi but her. More importantly, he admitted that her trying to save my job *when I didn't even need a job* made no sense to him. That, at least, was something positive.

Then came my big mistake with "tarts" when Anthony was about to tell me his alibi. What a huge mistake that was. Now how would I find out? There was no way I could return to his car lot. I'd have to check with Kasey to see if he ever came into the Kafe next door to the historical society. That place was a regular social bazaar. Or maybe more rightly put would be social bizarre.

Keeping my eyes closed and nodding my head at my progress —if you could call it that—I thought about my conversation with Elizabeth Conroy at the Rutledge Super Market. She thought Martha did it, and she even knew that Martha didn't want the sale to go through and it had nothing to do with me. I wish I could verify that with Martha, but it was a sensitive subject, and

I didn't want to bother her any more than she was already bothered. Elizabeth also said something else of interest. She admitted that *she* could be the murderer. What was that quote—of Oprah's, I think—"when someone tells you who they are, believe them." Had Elizabeth just confessed to me who she was? The murderer?

Anthony may or may not have an alibi which I "tarted" myself out of, so he would remain on my list, but Elizabeth? She now stood on the *top* of my list. Murderers don't always lie. Sometimes they tell the truth. And she said she could be the murderer. That was enough for me.

Suddenly I felt a hand on my shoulder. Opening my eyes, I looked up to see Billy looking down at me concerned. "Are you okay, Lor? Didn't you want to see the rest of the house? I thought you liked it?"

I reached down and pressed the button to return the chair to its regular position; and then I stood up and wrapped my arms around Billy. "I love it, Billy. There were some things that I needed to think about."

"I'm hoping it's not about the murder, Lorry, because I've got that covered."

Before I could admit or deny anything, he grabbed my hand to coax me down the hallway. "Come see our bedroom. You'll like it!"

Aiden grabbed my other hand and jumped up and down as we walked. "Mommy, my bedroom looks out over the horses! It's awesome!"

"That's great, sweetie. I'm glad you like it." Leaning over, I gave him a quick kiss on the top of his head. Luckily, he had quit jumping, or I might have timed it wrong and gotten a fat lip.

A fireplace, with vents and a glass front, built into the wall caught my attention as we walked into the spacious master bedroom. Have I told you how much I love fireplaces? Probably. There was a back door leading who knew where, and to the left of the door, attached to the ceiling and facing the bed, was another large television. We were not a television-loving family, but its sheer size still impressed me.

There were two dressers, matching night tables, and a king-size four poster bed with a red bedspread and matching black and red pillows that matched most of the throw rugs in the house. Right smack in the center of the bed, a solid black cat curled into himself, ignored us like we weren't even there.

"Oh, forgot to tell you. We inherited a cat. That's Tom."

I sneezed.

CHAPTER SEVENTEEN

"MOMMY, I THOUGHT you weren't allergic to cats anymore!"

"I'm not allergic to *Rocky*, anymore," I said, rubbing my itching eyes. I had decided not to be allergic to him, and it mostly worked. But this was a *new* cat. "And he's on our *bed*."

Billy stepped over. "You want me to get him off? I can do that, though I don't know how to keep him off unless we don't let him inside. But if that's what you want, Lor—"

"No, no, leave him alone and let him sleep. If I could get used to Rocky, I can get used to this one. What's his name again?"

"Tom."

"As in *tomcat*? If he's intact, we need to get him neutered right away," I said.

Billy hugged me. "Just a name, Lor, he's already taken care of." He squeezed me and turned to follow Aiden through a doorway to the right of the one we just came in. "Come on, Lor, and look how cool our bathroom is."

Although *cool* was not a word I'd use to describe a bathroom, I followed Aiden and Billy into it. To my left was a large area with two separate sinks.

"See this?" asked Billy. "His and hers sinks!"

"Nice!" I said. There were cabinets below and a large horizontal cabinet above, with sliding doors. To my right was a closet with plenty of space inside, and a matching closet on the other side of the entrance to the walk-in shower. I had never used one of those but had heard good comments about them. At the far side was a small room with the toilet.

"No bathtub?"

"You can use mine, Mommy. I'll share."

Billy shrugged and hugged Aiden. "No, just the one in the other bathroom. We can have one put in if you like."

Bingo moseyed out through the small dog door in the wall beside the toilet. "Where does it lead, Billy?"

"I think there's an enclosure outside." Bingo moseyed back into the room and looked up at me as if to say, "Nothing there, Mom." I leaned down and petted him, and he wagged his tail.

We exited the bathroom area and Bingo put two feet up on the bed to get a better sniff of the cat. The cat ignored him, so he jumped back down. Rocky at the historical society was Bingo's best friend. That made me think about something that I hadn't thought of before. What would happen to Rocky if they sold the historical society? One thing I knew for sure. No one would put that cat out on the street. I'd make sure of that. "I hope this cat gets along with other cats," I said.

"You thinkin' of getting another cat?"

I shook my head. "Just thinking, Billy, just thinking." But I somehow knew it would work out okay.

Aiden grabbed Billy's hand and pulled him toward the back door. "Let's go see the horses!"

Bingo and I followed them outside to a cement area leading to some stone footsteps in the direction of the big barn. And when I say *big barn*, I am not exaggerating one iota. It was huge—much bigger than our barn-wannabe gambrel house in town. I wanted to look inside, but Aiden was pointing out to the pasture and trying to pull Billy in that direction.

Walking past their backs toward the barn, I walked across a metal bridge that spanned a rock-lined ditch that I imagined was for drainage. Then I proceeded across a span of dead weeds and another metal bridge. Almost all the way across—it was only a yard long—one of my three-inch heels got caught between the bars of the bridge. So focused on pulling my heel out, I ignored the sound of a door opening. Trying to give the heel one last yank to get it free, I pitched forward and found myself in someone's arms. And the someone wasn't Billy.

The man set me on my feet and took a step back to look at me. And I took two steps back from him, covering myself as if I was naked and he had caught me coming out of the shower. Skinny as a fence post, the grizzled old cowboy in front of me had lines on his face from a lifetime of frowning.

"Who are you?" I asked in surprise. It wasn't exactly a question, though I wanted to know.

A grizzled old dog stood beside him and softly snarled, but the old man put his hand in the dog's face to quiet him. The retriever-sized dog had a long multi-colored coat. "I should be asking the same of you, ma'am." He said it politely but with an obvious edge.

Before I could tell the old codger off, Billy stepped up beside me and took my arm. Aiden, on the other side, held my hand.

"Ah, Bill," said the cowboy without smiling. "She belongs to you."

"Uncle Charlie, this is my wife, Lorry, and my son, Aiden. Lorry, Aiden, this is Uncle Charlie. He lives here."

Uncle Charlie took his well-worn black cowboy hat off and nodded his head to me. "Ma'am." Then he stuck out his hand for Aiden, who shook it enthusiastically.

"Can I pet your dog, Uncle Charlie?"

"No, boy. That's ole Buck. He and I prefer to keep to ourselves. Best leave him alone."

Ole Buck stood just behind Charlie softly growling. But he didn't move. Aiden came back and took my hand again.

"Uncle Charlie, would you mind if we looked at the bunkhouse?" Billy asked.

"No, go ahead. It's as clean as it's gonna get. Just don't touch the saddle!"

"Don't worry Uncle Charlie, we won't," said Billy, who led the way into the side entrance of the barn.

"Mommy?" Aiden said with his hand on the front of his pants. "I've gotta go."

"All right. We can go back to the house," I said as I turned around.

"Ma'am, he's welcome to use the toilet in the bunkhouse," Charlie said to me, and then to Aiden, he added, "Just don't pee on the seat, boy!"

"Thank you," I said.

Aiden pulled his hand out of mine, turned toward Charlie, and put both hands on his hips. "*I* don't pee on the seat! I urinate like a man!"

Charlie didn't smile at that, although it looked like his mouth wanted to. "I'll remember that, Aiden." He turned around and faded off into the sunset with the dog following, as the four of us strode into the barn.

CHAPTER EIGHTEEN

IT SMELLED LIKE a barn—in a good way. From my youth, I loved the smell of horses, and this brought back all those sweet horsey memories. Standing there, looking around at the vast interior of the barn, I didn't realize that Aiden was jumping up and down holding himself. Luckily, Billy noticed and showed him where the door to the bathroom was.

"It's huge in here," I remarked, thinking how silly that was. I mean, duh!

"Definitely a big barn," said Billy. "Let's look inside the bunkhouse before Uncle Charlie gets back. I don't want to bother him."

"Why do you call him *Uncle Charlie*? I know he's not really your uncle."

"Everybody calls him that."

"I'm not going to," I said, trying to moderate the defiant tone in my voice.

Billy shrugged. "Suit yourself," he said. "Here's Aiden now."

Aiden rubbed his hands on the front of his pants as he said, "Let's go see the horses!"

"Not yet, buddy boy. Didn't Uncle Charlie have towels in there?" Billy asked.

"Yeah, but I didn't think it was polite to use them, and I couldn't reach the paper towels hanging on the wall."

Billy pulled Aiden toward us, and we both hugged him. "What a great kid we've got!"

Aiden grabbed at Billy's hand and tried to pull him toward the wide front door of the barn. "Let's go see the horses, Daddy! We've seen enough of the inside of houses for today!"

I heard a little impatience seeping into his voice. I couldn't blame the kid. Looking at houses was boring compared to looking at horses. It made me realize that I wouldn't mind seeing the horses myself.

Billy looked at his watch, nodded, and said, "It's getting late. I need to get back. All right, we can see the bunkhouse another time. Let's go see the horses!"

We were about to see a whole lot more.

Billy led us through the long barn, past four half stalls and three double-size stalls, all set in the middle of the barn. Outside the stalls was enough room for a car to drive all the way around. There were no cars in the barn, though there was a big blue tractor in the front by the double barn doors that were wide open beckoning us toward the horses.

As we walked out into the late afternoon dim sunshine, Charlie and Buck approached us. Bingo stayed behind my legs, though Buck had never made one aggressive move toward him. Well, aside from baring his teeth at us humans.

"Hey, Bill," said Charlie, "you was going to let me know if it's all right to keep horses here or not." I cringed at his incorrect English, but if he lived here, there wasn't a lot I could do about it.

"What?" asked Aiden and looked at Billy.

Billy spoke to Aiden, "Uncle Charlie likes to buy and sell horses. If he does that, then he has to keep them here. What do you think about extra horses here?"

Aiden jumped up and down and nodded his head. "Yeah! More horses!"

"I guess that's a yes," Billy said to Charlie.

Charlie nodded his head. "Have you shown him the—" but he didn't get to finish because Billy held up his hand. "Ah, I see,"

75

said Charlie. "All right. I'll see y'all later." Without another word, Charlie and Buck walked past us down the long corridor to the bunkhouse. When he got past us, he grabbed hold of one of the stalls to keep from falling. Billy didn't notice it, but I did. Although I hadn't smelled alcohol on his breath, I'd bet he was an old drunk.

"Where's your horse, Daddy?"

"We're going to see him right now, little pard. And he has a friend."

"A friend?" asked Aiden, puzzled. "You mean another horse?"

"Well, another equine," said Billy.

"Equine?" asked Aiden. And I knew what his next library book would be about.

Billy took Aiden's hand and my hand, led us past two empty corrals, and toward the large pasture on the other side of the hay barn. When we got close and couldn't see anything, Billy asked us both to close our eyes, which we did. I wanted to peek, but if Aiden could do it, so could I.

He walked us a few more steps and through a gate. I heard him unhook the chain and re-hook it once we were on the other side. "Are you both ready?" asked Billy.

Aiden jumped up once. "Yes! Can we open our eyes?"

"Not yet," said Billy. Then he gave a long whistle.

We heard hoof beats approaching us fast, and I fought the urge to open my eyes. I trusted Billy.

"Almost," said Billy. "All right, you two. I'd like you to meet Spider and Spot. You can open your eyes now."

Spider, a tall, muscular black horse with two white front socks and a long black mane and tail, stood in front of Billy, nuzzling him. Behind Spider, not approaching too close, was Spot. And Spot was—a zebra.

CHAPTER NINETEEN

AIDEN, BUSY PETTING Spider's nose, didn't notice the zebra at first. When he looked up and saw it, he pointed and said, "Daddy! A zebra! You have a zebra!" He was about to take a leap in the zebra's direction when Billy held him back by the shoulder.

"No, you can't pet him, little pard. Spot is a little skittish right now. He might get used to you later." Billy had been so invested in showing us the house, barn, bunkhouse, and horses, that he had forgotten his time constraints. When he noticed the sun on its downward path, he said, "Oh, no! We need to leave right now or I'll be late, and that would be disastrous! Let's go!" He gave Spider one last stroke on his neck, called him a good boy, and then grabbed my and Aiden's hands and pulled us through the gate, pausing briefly to lock it. "C'mon! Run!" And Billy, Aiden, and Bingo ran for the truck, with me trying to keep up as best I could in my heels.

Billy and Aiden were already inside with their seat belts on when I arrived at the truck, huffing and puffing, and opened the door. Reaching over the seat, Billy offered me his hand and pulled me inside. Bingo was already on the seat waiting for me. Billy started the truck, and without hurrying, drove out the front gate, and down the narrow dirt road. When we got to the main road, he stepped on the gas, and the truck rattled and rolled across the potholes and washboard surface.

It was too uncomfortable riding in the truck to have much of a conversation, but Aiden tried. "Why is your horse named Spider, Daddy?"

"Because he has a peculiar marking on his right hip that looks like a spider hanging from a web." We rumbled over a deep rut bouncing all of us against our seat belts, and Billy said, "Oh, sorry."

"Why do you have a zebra?" Aiden asked.

"He kind of came with the house," said Billy, as we bumped along. "The people who left took all their horses with them, but they didn't want the zebra. And it's not good for horses to be all alone, so I bought the zebra so Spider would have company. It's called a *companion horse.*"

"Companion *zebra,* you mean," said Aiden.

"Yeah," laughed Billy.

"Are we going to sleep at the new house tonight?" asked Aiden.

"No, sweetie. We have a lot of moving in to do first. Plus, someone else needs to stay there for a while," said Billy.

"That old man, Uncle Charlie?"

"No, son. Uncle Charlie lives in the bunkhouse. Someone else. Listen, Aiden, I need to talk to your mother about that and about what's going on this evening. Everything you hear right now and everything you hear later has to stay with our family. Okay?"

"Sure, Daddy."

"Lor, I'll drop you off at the historical society and go straight to the Town Offices. After you lock up, drive there but don't come in. I'll call you on the car phone, because I know you forget to charge your cell phone half the time!" He glanced at me and smiled. "I'll call before I go in and leave my phone on speaker-phone in my pocket so you can hear everything that's going on. It will surprise you. Ah, here we are." Billy pulled smoothly onto the pavement from the rough road, past the barrier, and pulled up in front of the building in contention. "See ya soon. Love you both." He leaned over and kissed me.

Aiden, Bingo, and I got out, and Billy sped away. It was a couple of minutes past five, and Petra had already put the closed sign up. I unlocked the door, let us in, and was surprised to find Petra still behind her desk.

"Hey, Petra. Working late?"

"No, just studying."

"Want a ride home?" I asked as I hurried Aiden past her. When she said no, I was grateful, because it seemed like Aiden and I should get to the Town Offices soon. Stepping out the back door, the three of us piled into the car, and I drove over there. Since Billy said not to go in, I figured it might be better if my car wasn't seen, either, so I parked at the far end of the parking lot and didn't turn off the engine.

We hadn't been there a minute when the car phone rang. "Lor, I'm sticking the phone in my pocket now. Pay attention! Don't say anything while this phone is on! Love you!" I didn't even have a chance to say *I love you* back before I heard the faint rustle of Billy's shirt as the phone slid into his pocket.

CHAPTER TWENTY

I HEARD A door open and close and then some voices in the background, but I couldn't hear what they said. Aiden was leaning forward in the seat trying to hear, too. Even Bingo had his little ears pricked forward.

I could hear Billy's cowboy-booted feet walking, and I heard one of the council members say, "What are *you* doing here?" It sounded like Anthony Petrelli.

"I came to listen to the proceedings," said Billy. "And I was under the impression that these meetings were open to the public."

"How did you know we were meeting at five o'clock?" asked Elizabeth. "The public sessions start at six." The only reason I recognized her voice was because it wasn't Christa, so it had to be Elizabeth.

"Lucky guess," said Billy.

"We were about to vote on whether to discharge Martha Goldstein from her job as the town manager for malfeasance," said the mayor.

"I wouldn't do that if I were you," said Billy.

"We can do it if we want to!" said Anthony Petrelli. "Am I right or am I right?"

"I'm telling you, members of the High Council, with all due respect, I wouldn't do that." He had raised his voice just enough to get their attention.

"Sheriff Madrigal, this is town business and doesn't concern you."

I didn't know who it was until Aiden whispered, "That's Douglas Gates. He came to speak at our school."

Before Billy had a chance to say anything, another voice, so low we almost couldn't hear it, said, "Or you'll do what, Sheriff Madrigal?"

"Or I'll arrest *all* of you, that's what!" said Billy.

"You can't do that!" said Anthony Petrelli. "True or true?"

Billy laughed. "Of course I can do that! I'm the Sheriff!"

Although Aiden giggled from the back seat, the whole affair *scared* me. One of those people on the council was probably the killer. And Billy was baiting them. I had just gotten married, and I didn't want to be a widow.

I wondered why the mayor hadn't chimed in and then I heard his voice. "Sheriff Madrigal, you know you can't do that. It will never stick."

"You're right, mayor. It won't stick. But I can still bring you all in for twenty-four hours for questioning and maybe leak to the press that I had to arrest all the High Council. You'll all have a fun time living that one down."

"He can't do that, can he, mayor?" asked Douglas Gates.

I heard the door open and funny footsteps approach Billy, who sounded like he stood in front of the council. The footsteps were funny because it was two steps and a third—it was Wichita Wiggins and his cane. His voice boomed out next. "Of course he can do it! And I sanction his actions! What y'all are doing to that woman—do you know what it's called? It's called slander. And if the papers get hold of it and quote any of you or *think* they have quoted any of you, then it is libel. And you're in a heap o' trouble.

"So, as your designated town attorney, I would advise you to drop the notion of firing Martha. There has been no malfeasance here, except the murder, which I have no reason to believe she is any more guilty—or innocent—than any of *you*." After a hesitation he added, "Russell, make sure you get all this down."

There was a muffled response, and I heard grumbling on the council. I couldn't distinguish any voices—it was all more like a jumble of disconnected words. They sounded angry.

"And I'd like to advise you," I heard Billy's voice say, "that if you call this meeting to order at another time and this subject is revisited, I will carry out what I did not do tonight. But I *will* come to each of your businesses—*after* I call the newspaper—and arrest each and every one of you, handcuffs and all. Except for you, mayor, and that's only because there is no way you could have done it. Although I could still bring you in for questioning."

"That's a threat!" yelled Anthony Petrelli, and I could picture him shaking his fist in the air. He was an annoying little man who thought he was a big shot. "Am I right or am I right?"

"No, you're not right, Anthony. That's a fact," said Wichita.

"Do I have a motion to adjourn the meeting?" asked the mayor.

"I move that we adjourn the meeting," said Elizabeth Conroy.

"I second the motion," said Douglas Gates.

"Meeting adjourned," said the mayor.

Then I heard the jumble of disconnected words again and chairs moving across the floor. The meeting was adjourned.

"One more thing, council," said Billy. "I have arranged that Martha will take some time off, so she doesn't have to hear any of these comments around town."

"She can't leave town! She is still under suspicion like the rest of us! No matter what you think!" Anthony Petrelli said, and it sounded like he was right in Billy's face. "And you know that's true!"

"She will not be leaving town, but she will be inaccessible. I'll know where she is and Wichita will know where she is. Nobody else needs to know," said Billy.

"It sounds like you're protecting her," said Douglas Gates.

"Yes! I'm protecting her from the likes of all of you! She is too nice a lady to hear all the rumors that all of you are spreading around town."

"I know we've already adjourned the meeting, but I think the rest of the council will agree with me, this is not a paid leave for Martha," said the mayor.

Billy sighed. I could even hear it in the phone. "It will be vacation time, mayor. And it might interest you to know that's the first thing Martha said to me when I suggested her taking time off. 'I won't take paid leave. I'll take vacation time.' *That's* the kind of woman you're accusing of malfeasance."

"She's still a suspect, though, right?" asked Elizabeth.

"Yes, Elizabeth. She's still a suspect. Just like *you.*" It sounded nasty, but I could tell that he had a smile in his voice. He must like Elizabeth, despite what happened at the meeting. "And if I find any kind of evidence that she is the perpetrator, I will haul her in just like the rest of you," Billy said it to the room, not to one single person. I could tell by the projection in his voice.

I heard many sets of footsteps filing out of the room, and Billy and Wichita were silent. Aiden whispered from the back seat, "Did he turn off the phone?"

"I don't think so. I didn't hear it click."

"Thanks, Wichita, for coming tonight and supporting me," said Billy.

"Well, you and I know she didn't do it, but she does need to stay on the suspect list. Where is she going to be?"

"My new place—just inside town limits," Billy said. Then we heard a click and the connection was cut off. We had heard what Billy wanted us to hear, and I appreciated him for that.

CHAPTER TWENTY-ONE

DECIDING NOT TO wait for Billy to come out of the town offices, we drove home. Since Billy was talking to Wichita, he could be a while. Thinking over the conversation and *drama* I just heard, I didn't know where Billy would start his investigation, but I knew where I would continue mine. And that would happen tomorrow.

"Mommy?" Aiden asked before we got home. "Can we have pizza for dinner? I'm hungry."

"Sure, baby. Let's wait for Daddy to get home."

"Mommy, he and Wichita could talk all night." Aiden knew about Billy's long-winded conversations with Wichita.

I laughed. "You're so right, Aiden. We'll see when we get home."

It didn't take long. We weren't home five minutes before Billy arrived carrying a hot pizza. Sometimes, I swear, that man reads my mind.

When we sat down to eat, between mouthfuls of pepperoni pizza, Billy asked, "So what did you think?"

"I think you did something incredibly kind for Martha. But Billy, I also think you took a big risk for yourself." I put my hand on his arm. "One of those people is probably the murderer, and you provoked him tonight."

"Yeah, Daddy," Aiden piped in, "I don't want to lose you. You're the only Daddy I've ever known."

Billy put one hand out to me and one to Aiden and patted us both. "Don't worry. I can take care of myself; and I had Wichita there to support me. It will be fine."

"I hope so," I said. "So Martha will be at the new house with Hugo?"

"Martha will be there alone for a few days. Hugo has to stay for some guests that have reservations at their bed and breakfast."

"Will Martha be okay out there all alone?"

"Yeah, why not?"

"Well, you know, that Charlie man. And his vicious dog."

"Oh, Lorry, you worry too much. Buck isn't vicious, and he's never out on his own. Uncle Charlie is fine. He's very responsible. I've never known him to shirk any of his duties."

"I think he's a drunk, Billy."

"Oh, I don't think so. He used to be an alcoholic, but he's been on the wagon for years."

"I know you didn't notice, but I saw him weaving as he walked."

"Whatever," said Billy, waving my worry away, "Martha will be fine out there."

"All right. I hope so." Stuffing more pizza into my mouth, I nodded. "You going to take her out there tomorrow?"

"Um, well, I was hoping you would."

Frowning, I began to say that I already had plans, but since I didn't want Billy to know about them, I hesitated and said, "Sure." I hoped that Billy heard the word more than my hesitation.

"Great," he said, more involved in eating the pizza than the details of the conversation. "You can call her tomorrow to arrange when to pick her up."

"Yeah, sure," I said, wondering if I could leave Petra alone twice while I took Martha to the new house *and* proceeded with my investigation.Work had slowed down since all the excitement over the new exhibit. Still, Petra had her schoolwork to do. All I could do was ask and see what she said. So I ate another slice of pizza.

For the rest of the evening, we didn't talk about Martha or what happened at the meeting. We watched one of Aiden's movies and discussed the new house. We made plans that I would start packing, but I still wasn't willing to accept the notion of selling my wonderful gambrel house. That decision would have to wait until later. W had plenty of time and plenty of money, so it didn't matter, anyway.

When the movie finished, Aiden asked, "When can I ride the zebra, Dad?"

Billy laughed. "*Nobody* rides Spot, Aiden. We'll get you and your Mom—if she wants one—two good horses."

"Aiden should have a pony, not a horse. He's only seven."

"No! I want a horse! I'm almost eight!"

"You won't be eight for six more months, Aiden," I said.

"You'll have to talk to Uncle Charlie about the wisdom of getting a pony," said Billy.

"A horse is too big for him," I said.

"I want a horse!" said Aiden, who stuck out his lower lip and crossed his arms across his little chest. I'm not necessarily proud that he learned that from me, but on him, it looked cute.

"We'll discuss it after your mom talks to Uncle Charlie. He has a lot of connections and will come up with something good for the two of you." He looked at me. "You want a horse, *don't you*? You know, so we can all ride together."

I looked off into space thinking about horses and their connection to my trip to the Grand Canyon. And then I thought about the mules at the Grand Canyon and how my experience with horses had made me comfortable with them. So horses had been my key away from my abusive marriage to Eddie. They changed my life. A tear dribbled out of one of my eyes. I think it was the left one. It must have been, because Billy noticed it, and he was sitting to my left. Bingo, who was at my feet, looked up at me and whined.

"Are you okay, Lorry? You don't have to get a horse if you don't want to."

I tried surreptitiously to wipe the tear away, although there was nothing surreptitious about it because Billy was looking straight at me. So I smiled to ease the fearful look he gave me. "I would *love* to have a horse," I said. And I meant it.

CHAPTER TWENTY-TWO

THE FOLLOWING MORNING, I got to the office before Petra, which, while it wasn't a first, was probably a second or third. She almost always arrived before me—already finished with work and engaged in her studying. So that surprised me.

I called Martha and arranged to pick her up at ten o'clock. Since I didn't think I'd be gone long, I thought Petra would be okay with it. She usually was. Whether I got to go on my other errand of investigating the murder didn't matter as much as taking care of Martha and making sure she got settled in the new ranch house.

At nine-fifteen, Petra stumbled in the door. Her eyes had that deer-in-the-headlights look, her make-up was smeared, her blouse untucked, and even one of her pierced earrings was missing. I'd never seen her like that. She staggered past me and past her office.

"Petra? You okay?" I didn't want to mention her looks, because she must have known. Maybe that's why she was heading to the bathroom.

"Yeah, fine," I heard her say before she closed the door to the bathroom. Her voice sounded weird.

A few minutes later, she walked—it sounded normal—back to her desk. I heard her sit down and turn on her computer.

"Petra?" I asked. "Is everything all right?"

"Yeah, fine. I'm fine. Perfectly fine." Normally, she would say that with an edge to it because I annoyed her. This time, though, she said it in a flat monotone voice. I thought it sounded like when you asked people *How are you?* and even though they have a broken arm, they say *fine* from habit or something.

"Um, I hate to ask this when you're feeling stressed or whatever, but do you mind if I take off this morning for a while? I have to take Martha out to the new house. Billy wanted to protect her from all the rumors running around town. Do you mind?"

"Yeah, yeah, sure. Take your time. I wouldn't mind being alone all day today. You have anything else to do? Just do it. It hasn't been busy, and I'm fine. Really fine."

She didn't sound fine at all. Her voice didn't have her usual spark in it, though it sounded sincere. Kind of. And besides, I wanted to do that other errand. Looking back on this, I should have paid more attention.

"Okay, thanks. I appreciate that. I'll get back when I get back." I don't think she heard the thanks or the other comment, because I heard her whispering into her phone. She usually talked that way to Mason. It must be him.

Petra said nothing else. A while later, I could hear the keys of her computer clacking away, so I figured she must be working and back to normal. I hoped she had tucked in her blouse, but I didn't think I should ask.

While I was waiting to go pick up Martha, an idea that had been rumbling around in my brain occurred to me, so I placed a call to Bryan O'Keefe, my attorney. I had met Bryan a few months earlier when I was accused of murder. The exact place where I met him—I'm more than embarrassed to say—was in the holding cell at the Sheriff's station where *Billy* had put me. Although we weren't married then or even dating, it still wasn't a great memory. Bryan had been great, and now we were all great friends. Bryan and his partner, Ryan, sometimes babysat for Aiden when Billy and I had our rare night out. Bryan didn't answer the phone, so I left a message for him to call me back.

Just before I had to leave to pick up Martha, the front door jingled and opened, and in walked Zack James with a concerned look on his face.

"Lorry!" He smiled and hugged me.

The first time I met Zack, he was in jail, and I was talking to him through a computer set-up at the Coyote Moon jail. He was a former juvenile delinquent who I had somehow extricated from his jail cell by my astute observation of detail. At least that's how I'd put it. Billy would put it another way. Zack was grateful just the same. "How are you, kiddo?" I asked when we pulled apart from the hug.

"Doing great, Lorry, thanks to you." After they released him from jail, he cleaned up his act, got a job cleaning the local post office, and took college classes in the evening. Then, one of his professors was so impressed that he got him a computer job, and Zack quit the post office. His life was improving in leaps and bounds, and he thought he owed it all to me. He didn't, and I kept trying to tell him that, but he liked to attribute his success to me. Zack says I believed in him which made him believe in himself.

"How's your new job? You miss the post office?"

"Hardly at all," he smiled at me and poked me in the arm, but I could see he was inching his way toward Petra's office.

"Well, good to see you, Zack!"

"Good to see you, too, Lorry." And he was one speed short of running into the next room.

I stood up to leave and as I walked out the door, I could see Petra in his arms, and he was *comforting* her. It looked like her shoulders were shaking, so she was either laughing or crying, and considering how she looked earlier, I figured it was crying.

Although Zack had feelings for her since before jail, she only considered him a good friend. Mason was her tried-and-true boyfriend. But Mason lived in Flagstaff. Still, I didn't know what this was about. I said nothing and closed the door softly behind me.

CHAPTER TWENTY-THREE

MARTHA AND HUGO were lugging her suitcases out of the house when I arrived. I got out to help them put them into the back of my car. "Are you taking everything you own?" I joked.

Martha and Hugo looked at each other and frowned. "We don't know how long I'll have to stay there," said Martha.

"Oh, I'm sorry, Martha. I didn't mean to joke. This is serious, isn't it?"

Hugo put his arm around Martha. "We've never been apart for more than a day," he said, blinking away the tears that wanted to pour from his eyes.

Martha turned, gave Hugo a big hug, kissed him on the mouth, and said, "Let's go. I can't stand this." She walked to the passenger side of the car where she pulled a tissue out of her purse and blew her nose.

"I'm sorry, Hugo." I hugged him.

"Not your fault, Lorry. It's the town's people. What I don't understand is how they could think my Martha could do that."

"What I think happened, Hugo, is the killer started the rumor, and everyone else picked up on it. Once Billy finds the killer, everything will be put right again."

"I hope so. I hate this," said Hugo.

Then Martha honked the horn in my car, and when we looked over at her, she raised her hands palm upwards. That wasn't anything like Martha would normally do. She must really feel stressed. And who could blame her?

I noticed that Bingo, who had been sitting in the passenger seat, had climbed onto Martha's lap and was licking her chin. That dog knows when he's needed.

After kissing Hugo on the cheek, I opened the door of the car, slid in, and started it. "Sorry, Martha."

"I'm sorry, Lorry. I'm so stressed over this ridiculous situation. And I even had a feeling that Billy didn't want me to get away from town to protect me from the rumors but to *protect* me. That scares me. What if the bad person doesn't realize I'm not at home now? What if he sets fire to our house or something?"

"Everyone on the town council knows. Billy made sure of that. And the only other suspect is the son." I thought for a minute and made up my mind. "And I'll make sure he knows. Not to worry, Martha." I patted her on the hand.

"What about the other people in the audience? I know Petra and Mason didn't do it, but there were a few others there."

"I'll find out, Martha. Don't worry. Hugo and your house will be fine." I didn't know that for sure, but I had to say something to comfort her, didn't I?

She looked at me and put her hand on my arm as we drove past the barrier and out onto the dirt road leading to our new house. "Do you think you could get Billy to ask Nick to park in front of the house to make sure nobody does anything?"

"Martha, if Billy thought your house was in danger, he would do that without asking." When a low moan and a hiccup escaped from Martha, I told her, "I will ask him about that when I get back to the office. Okay? Will that make you feel better?"

She nodded. "A lot better."

We'd driven a mile in silence when I thought of something and pulled over to the side of the road. "Martha! You need groceries out there! We need to turn around and go to the market."

"No, Lorry, don't bother. Billy already took care of that for me. I gave him a list, and he asked some man to do it and deliver them. I'll have plenty to eat."

"Who was the man? That Charlie guy?"

"Uncle something is what Billy said. Yeah, it might have been Charlie."

"You be careful of him, Martha. Him and that vicious dog of his."

"Billy trusts him. And he went out of his way to get me these groceries. Maybe he's nicer than you think, Lorry. You worry too much."

What she didn't say, and could have, is that I was judging the Charlie character without even knowing him. I'm trying, and I'm much better than I used to be. Besides, sometimes you have to judge people, don't you? I mean, some people are begging to be judged. Aren't they?

I pulled back out onto the dirt road, turned my head, and gave her a look. Suddenly she realized what she had said and how worried she had been about her house. She started laughing, and I started laughing, and we couldn't stop. The sad part was that the laughing turned into crying for Martha. She got out another tissue from her purse, wiped her eyes, and blew her nose. Bingo started licking her face again. And she let him.

"This is a pretty drive out here, isn't it Martha?" I said, trying to distract her from the ugly truth of her being separated not only from the husband and home she loved, but from her job that I knew she enjoyed.

"Very pretty. However did Billy find this place?"

"He boards his horse out here."

"Do you ride, too?"

I smiled, thinking of fond horsey memories. "Yup." Then I realized this was the perfect time to tell Martha about Eddie and the Grand Canyon and horses. Although she knew a lot of my secrets, this was one I had never told her. So I began the story.

CHAPTER TWENTY-FOUR

"EDDIE SOMEHOW GOT the idea that he wanted to take a vacation to the Grand Canyon. Considering what happened afterward, I think he had planned the whole thing, but this is how it went.

"I didn't want to go, but as usual he got his way. When we got there and had to get on the mules, Eddie was scared. And even though riding down that steep canyon path sounded scary to me before we got there, since I had ridden horses before, once we got there, it turned out that I was the brave one. That gave me confidence.

"After we had been to the bottom of the canyon and were on our way back—his mule was behind mine—Eddie yells out, 'You know, Lorry, your butt is bigger than that mule's, and I'm tired of following it. As soon as we get home, I'm leaving!'

"When we got to the top, Eddie went to the restroom, and I drove the car home and left him there with no transportation! I got lucky, though. When Eddie said that, I reacted with confidence instead of fear. If it hadn't come down exactly as it had, I'd probably still be with him now. And I attribute it all to my experience with horses. So, in a way, horses saved my life, and I'll always feel grateful for that.

"Oh, here we are." I turned the car left on Sylvan Way, continued through the entrance of the ranch, and parked in front of the double-car garage.

"Wow, it's big."

"It isn't all house. The garage separates the house from this little apartment over there." I motioned with my arm toward the apartment.

"And the barn is huge, too." Martha said, still looking all around her.

"Yes, it is. There's a bunkhouse in there—that's where Charlie lives. It's small and takes up very little room. Come on in, let's get you settled." I opened the door of the car, walked to the back, and opened it up. Before Martha saw me, I took a quick glance at my watch. I'd hoped to get back to the office in time to go out again and continue my investigation.

Pulling Martha's belongings out of the back of the car, I set them on the ground. Then the two of us picked everything up and walked to the front door of the house. When we got there, I stopped short.

"Oh, no," I said. "Billy forgot to give me a key."

Martha brightened. "He gave me one!" She set her luggage down and started digging through her purse.

While I waited, I tried the front door. The knob turned, and it opened. That didn't seem very safe to me, but I said nothing to Martha.

"Here we go. He must have left it open for us." Opening the door, I let Martha in while I looked around to make sure no one saw us entering without using a key. It wasn't that I didn't want them to think we were sneaking in—I didn't want anyone else to know that the door had been left unlocked. Since there were no houses anywhere in sight, I had nothing to worry about. I'd have to get used to living way out here in the boonies.

We entered, and I locked the door. "Martha, this way. Let me show you to your room." I led her down the hallway and pointed out Aiden's bedroom, the bathroom, the guest bedroom, and when I entered the master bedroom—where Billy told me Martha was to stay—she wasn't behind me anymore.

After setting her luggage down on the floor, I said, "Martha? Where'd ya go?"

I retraced my steps and found her in the guest bedroom. "What are you doing here?"

"This is the guest room. I'm a guest."

"No, no, no, no, no. Billy gave me strict instructions that you were to stay in the master bedroom and not to take no for an answer." I picked up the luggage she had set down and walked into the master bedroom.

Martha reluctantly followed. "Oh, Lorry, I can't take your bedroom. That's not right."

"Martha, we don't even live here yet! I only saw the house for the first time yesterday!"

Bingo had put his feet up on the bed trying to smell Tom the cat who lay sprawled in the middle of the bed again. Martha knelt down and said, "Who's this? Is he friendly?"

"That's Tom. He came with the house. I'm not sure."

Martha started stroking him, and he stood up rubbing himself against her. "I guess he's friendly," she said. "At least I won't be alone here."

I swallowed hard and coughed out the words, hoping Martha wouldn't notice my hesitation. "Would you like to keep Bingo with you while you're here? You're welcome to." I hadn't even had Bingo back a year yet and volunteering to leave him with Martha, even for a few days, felt worse than getting a root canal. I've never had a root canal, but I know they feel bad. That's why I said that. You know what I mean.

Martha stood up. "No, Lorry. No need. I won't be here that long, and I have Tom." She looked at the cat and smiled. Then she looked around the room. "Which dresser do you want me to use?"

"They're all empty. Take your pick!" I pointed into the bathroom area. "The bathroom and closets with hangers are in there. Make yourself at home. Do whatever you want!"

Suddenly grabbing me and hugging me, Martha started crying again. "Oh, Lorry, thank you so much for taking care of me like this. You and Billy. What would I do without you?"

"Are you kidding? After what you did for me when I first moved to town?" Martha had given me an advance, let me live in her bed and breakfast, and treated me like family. She *was* family to me—the *good* kind of family—not like the kind of family that I grew up with.

CHAPTER TWENTY-FIVE

AFTER HELPING MARTHA unpack all her suitcases and checking the refrigerator to make sure everything she wanted was there, Bingo and I walked out to the car. Martha waved from the doorway, and she looked so sad that it made me want to cry. But it wasn't my doing that caused her to be here—it was the council. And I hated them for what they were doing to her.

Halfway home, my cell phone rang, and I pulled over so I could answer. It was Bryan. I told him what I wanted, and he said he'd take care of it for me. And I knew he would. He was like that. And I was grateful he didn't call while Martha was in the car. This was something I wanted to keep secret for now. I wasn't even going to tell Billy or Aiden yet. When the time was right, and everything was set, then I would. There's a timing to things, you know?

The rest of the drive was long and bumpy. I wondered how it would feel when I had to make that long drive everyday. It was probably hard on my car. Maybe I could get another car or a truck. But I loved my car. Wait! I could have both! And maybe a Cadillac, too!

When you've been living paycheck to paycheck for so long—and it was always paycheck to paycheck with Eddie—it was difficult to get used to being a gazillionaire. I had been so used to trying to figure out if I could fill up the car with gas or if I should just get a couple of gallons to make sure I could get some groceries.

It was a hard way to live, but in retrospect (although I was glad it was in retrospect), I think it was a good experience. It taught me to appreciate money and that lack of money is not always due to someone spending wildly—sometimes it's out of their control. I suppose you could say Eddie gambling and spending *my* hard-earned money was in my control. That wasn't so. He told me every day how stupid I was and that no one else would ever want me. How could I leave? And when you hear those comments every day like that, you begin to believe them. And the more you hear them, the more you believe that they're true.

I shook my head to get rid of those horrible thoughts of my yesterdays, crossed to the other side of the barrier, and pulled my car in front of the historical society. "I'll be right back, Bingo," I said, as I patted him on the head. Stepping out of the car, I looked at him again. "Oh, maybe you better stay here with Petra. Would you mind?" I asked him. Looking out at the street to make sure there were no cars coming, I called him out of the car. We walked into the historical society together.

"It's me. Don't get up," I called. I didn't want to disturb Petra any more than I had to.

Walking into her office, I braced myself for what she might look like, but she had cleaned herself up. She had tucked in her blouse, and the smeared make-up had been fixed. Except I could tell that she had been crying, because there were tear tracks down her cheeks.

Putting everything together—Petra crying, Zack comforting her—it was obvious what had happened: she and Mason had broken up. Hadn't Mason just emailed me a chess cartoon like everything was normal? Sometimes he does that because once upon a time I used to be a chess master. Yes, that cartoon *was* this morning. It was a cartoon with two men facing each other across a chess table, with the timer on the table, and one of the two guys says something about not taking the game seriously. And when you look closer, the other guy has a pawn stuck up his nose. If Petra and Mason had broken up, would Mason send me something so flippant?

There was no way to know with Petra, and I didn't think it was my place to ask. But I did have to ask her something. "Would you mind if I took off again? It won't be too long. And would you mind babysitting Bingo?"

She looked at me with a serious expression on her face. I don't think she realized about the tear stains on her cheeks. "Lorry, if you could find somewhere to disappear today, I would appreciate it very much. So leave for as long as you want." Petra leaned down, picked Bingo up, and put him into her lap. It was the first time I had seen her smile all day. "As for Bingo, he is welcome here anytime!" A tear slipped down her cheek, but I pretended I didn't see it.

Not knowing what else to say or even if saying anything was appropriate, I said, "Thank you for taking care of Bingo. Bye." And I walked out the front door to my car. Again I thought it a better idea to walk than drive. It was brisk out, though not too bad. The sun was shining. So I pulled my car around the corner and into the alley and parked behind the historical society. Then I grabbed my purse and set off in the direction of my investigation. I shouldn't call it an investigation, though. If Billy found out, he would not be happy with me. But a girl's gotta do what a girl's gotta do. Right?

CHAPTER TWENTY-SIX

AFTER FIVE MINUTES of walking, I entered through the big automatic double doors of Rutledge Super Market. This time I decided to dispense with pretending I was shopping and go straight to Brent Lindsay's office in the back of the store. So I strolled back there with my head held high like I owned the place. Not that I *wanted* to own the place—I didn't—but I could if I wanted to. And realizing that is an interesting feeling. One never knows how one's circumstances can change so quickly. But they can. That's a good lesson for the masses. Things change. That's how life is. This, too, shall pass, and all that.

Brent was on the phone when I got there—I could see him through the big glass window into his office. So instead of staring in at him, I looked in at the meat display, particularly Maine lobster and Atlantic Salmon. The lobster would be good for a special treat, but I wouldn't dare buy the Atlantic Salmon. Aiden had said if I brought it home and tried to serve it, he would knock it to the floor and stomp it with both feet. Yes, he really said that. He's a good kid but very passionate about what he believes, and he believes that Atlantic Salmon—farmed salmon —is not healthy for you. So I've never even tried to serve it.

That's because of Aiden, not because of the unhealthy part. I mean, unhealthy is relative, isn't it? A hot fudge sundae? What could be bad about something that makes you feel so good? Don't ask me, because I don't know. And pizza? It has all the food groups in it, right? So that makes it the *perfect* food, not junk food!

Brent Lindsay stepped up beside me and interrupted my reverie. "Lorry? You here to shop or to see me? I wouldn't ask, except this is a strange hour for you to be shopping for groceries."

Brent Lindsay was a tall, thin, attractive man in his mid-fifties. His dark hair and mustache reminded me of the villain in that melodrama skit about not paying the rent. But he was so straight-forward and logical that I couldn't help but like him. So instead of making something up which would have sounded made up, I told him the truth. "Yes, I'm here to see you. I just wanted your take on the murder and on everyone blaming Martha."

"Not everyone is blaming Martha. I'm not. I don't think for a second that she did it." He folded his arms across his chest and leaned against the wall between the meat counter and the window to his office. "You might have noticed—or your husband might have told you—that I wasn't at the meeting where they gathered to condemn Martha. I didn't want any part of it."

I liked him even better. "No, I didn't know that. Even the mayor thinks she's guilty, though, and he's known her for years."

"I'm not sure if Joe really thinks she did it or is just going along with it because that's the quickest way to get through this. And I don't think he's the only one who thinks like that."

Thinking back over my previous conversations, I had to agree with him. The most expedient choice. That's what Elizabeth had said. So I nodded my head and raised my eyebrows hoping that would encourage him to go on.

"Do you know if I was the only one who didn't show?" he asked. Then he shook his head. "No, you probably don't if you didn't even know I wasn't there."

"Doesn't everybody have to be present to pass a resolution or a motion or whatever it's called?"

"No, definitely not. There has to be a quorum—the majority of the members present—and then if the majority of the quorum agree to something, it's a done deal. It's a little more complicated than that—they have special town council rules, but basically that's it. So they didn't need me to do their dirty work."

"And it is dirty work, too, blaming poor Martha. She wouldn't hurt a fly!" When he nodded his head, I asked, "So who do you think did it?"

This time he shook his head, put his arms down at his sides, and said, "I have no idea. I just know it wasn't me." And then, without saying another word, he turned and walked back into his office.

Everything was going so well, and then there at the end with what he said, how he said it, his body language, and his abrupt departure, I could only surmise one thing: he did it. He just shot up to the top of my list.

Instead of walking back down the alley, I crossed the street at High, and proceeded to the Rutledge Koffee Korner Kafe. Kasey might have some new information I could use.

I strolled through the open door and sat myself down at the counter by the cash register. Kasey was there taking someone's money. When the person stepped away from the counter, Kasey looked at me.

"Did you come to ask me questions or to buy something?"

Since honesty had worked with Brent Lindsay, I decided to try it with Kasey. She'd know I wasn't telling the truth, anyway, as soon as I asked a question. Or two. Or three.

"Both," I replied. "Coffee and a croissant. And do you ever see Anthony Petrelli in here?"

She shook her head as she turned around to pick up the carafe of coffee. As she poured it, she said, "Never." When she handed me the croissant, she asked, "So I suppose you want the rundown on the rest of the council members. Is that it?"

Why not, I thought. As long as she was asking—and hopefully willing—I may as well take advantage of the situation. "No, not all of them. Just a few." Before she could complain, I spilled the rest out. "Paul Gallagher, Russ Tabor, and Douglas Gates. And I wouldn't mind knowing if you ever see Fenton's son, Todd."

She put her hands on her hips, narrowed her eyes, and glared at me. Then she erupted. "Believe me, Lorry, if I had seen that little twerp Todd Fenton, I would sic you right on him. If the sale goes through, I most certainly will lose my job! And I need this job! John and I are talking about having another child."

That surprised me. I knew John wanted one, but I thought maybe he'd changed his mind after what had, um, happened between them. Nodding, I took a sip of my coffee and a bite of the croissant. "Okay," is all I could think of to say. I'm not always witty and articulate.

"Paul Gallagher usually stops by first thing in the morning before he heads to the high school. Tabor is a reclusive. Nobody ever sees him anywhere but at the town office. And Douglas Gates doesn't drink coffee. He prefers the *hard* stuff."

At that moment, several people walked into the Kafe, and Kasey put a smile on her face—that looked genuine—and walked around the counter to seat them and give them menus. It took a minute to absorb that until I realized Kasey must really like her job. That had never occurred to me before. Another assumption on my part. It wasn't a job I would like, so I had assumed Kasey didn't like it, either. As I gathered up my coffee and croissant, I turned around to look at the family who had come in. There was a father, a mother, a little girl of seven, and a nine-year-old boy who looked like he was on speed.

So many kids do these days. Between electronic devices and too much sugar, most of them look like they're hopped up on something. This kid was sitting down, standing up, sitting down, standing on the chair, sitting on the chair, ad infinitum. Or ad nauseam. One of the two. Probably both. I left money on the counter, waved to Kasey, and walked out the door.

CHAPTER TWENTY-SEVEN

WHEN I WALKED into the historical society, Bingo greeted me at the door. After placing the coffee and the croissant on my desk, I knelt down to pet him. What a good boy! Bingo was the love of my life until Aiden and Billy had come into it. But Bingo still stayed high up there.

I stood up from petting Bingo and sat down at my desk. Looking at the croissant, which I didn't really want, I stood back up. Stand up, sit down, stand up—I was as bad as the kid next door. Walking into Petra's office, I started to ask if she wanted the croissant—"Petra"—but I didn't get to finish because she had her face in her hands, crying. "Petra, what's wrong? Are you all right?" I set the croissant on her desk and put my hand on her shoulder. Don't worry. The croissant was in a napkin and my hands were clean, so I didn't soil her bright-colored blouse.

She waved me away with one hand while keeping her face covered with the other. "It's that family who just left here. You could tell the father and daughter had a good relationship—you know—that he was a good dad."

I nodded and patted her on the shoulder again to show my understanding. Since she was born, Petra's father had been an alcoholic and had *never* been a good dad. He had even beaten up on her mother for a while. I thought that had stopped, though. "Want to talk about it?" I offered, knowing she would never accept. Petra normally kept family stuff to herself. Whether she felt embarrassed or thought it was an inappropriate subject, I didn't know. There was no way to know since Petra wouldn't talk about it.

Petra waved me away again, sniffled, and turned back to her computer. But when Bingo jumped up on the side of her chair, she turned and let him nuzzle her. Bingo could comfort anyone. It was one of his awesome qualities.

Returning to my desk, I checked my email, drank the last of the coffee, and trudged down the hallway toward the stairs. Sneaking a quick glance at Petra, she faced her computer and typed madly away, but her shoulders shook as if she was controlling sobs. If she wouldn't let me in, then I couldn't help her. I tried to nudge Bingo to go to her again, but he wanted to follow me upstairs. Poor Petra. Probably her breakup with Mason had caused her to be more sensitive to other issues. In retrospect, I had that half right.

Sitting at my upstairs computer, I mindlessly scanned documents so we could—at some time in the future—put all the files online. If the historical society had any future, that is. Not knowing if that would ever happen because of the way things now stood, my heart wasn't in it. Time buzzed by, and I scanned and scanned. It wasn't long before I heard Aiden coming up the stairs, and Bingo raced from my side to meet him on the stairs.

A minute later, Aiden sat on my lap, with Bingo at my feet, and Rocky rubbing up next to Bingo and purring so loudly that Aiden and I had to raise our voices. It was okay, though, we all loved Rocky and put up with his cattiness.

Aiden told me about his day at school, and it was a welcome respite from the rest of my day talking to Brent Lindsay and Kasey. After a while, though, when he finished his stories and comments of his time at school, he climbed off my lap and onto the floor. There, with both Bingo and Rocky somehow squeezing onto his lap, he began to read. Sometimes he sat in Petra's office, but I was glad he didn't today. I didn't want him to bother her. Grieving over a lost relationship was always a difficult thing to do, and even more so if you were only sixteen years old.

When five o'clock came, Aiden and I packed up our belongings, and shuffled down the stairs. I said, "Bye, Petra!" and Aiden called out, "Bye, Petra! I love you!" I thought I heard her draw in her breath, but I probably imagined that. She never responded to our comments. Maybe she was on the phone.

I hadn't spoken to Billy all afternoon, so it surprised me when he was already home when we got there. Walking into the house, we found him in the kitchen with his *Kiss the Chef* apron on, and dinner on the table.

Doing as I was told (from the apron), I kissed him on the lips and told him I'd be right back. Color me hungry. Then I changed my clothes as fast as I could, washed my hands, and hurried back into the kitchen. Dinner smelled wonderful! Aiden was already sitting at the table. I wrapped my arms around Billy. "Have I told you lately what a great husband you are?"

Billy grinned. "Not enough!" He served the meat loaf and broccoli and sat down to join us.

The delicious meat loaf had parsley, red peppers, and spices in it. The three of us scarfed it down without much talking. We were all hungry! Although I told him Martha's concerns about the danger to the bed and breakfast, Billy assured me everyone on the council , the audience, *and* Todd Fenton knew she was out of town.

When we finished cleaning up, Billy said, "Okay, gang. Let's go!"

"Where are we going, Daddy?" asked Aiden.

"Packing! We are packing to get ready to move into our new home!"

"Yay!" said Aiden, jumping up and down and clapping.

"What about Martha?" I asked.

"She'll move back home as soon as I solve the murder."

My eyes sparkled. "Do you have any leads?" I tried to suppress the enthusiasm in my voice.

Billy shrugged. "Not yet, but I'm sure I'll come up with something as the investigation proceeds." He turned and began walking down the hallway. "Come on. The boxes are already in place, and we can begin."

I had noticed Billy had put boxes in our bedroom, but I was in too much of a hurry to eat dinner to pay much attention. Aiden walked into his bedroom, and I followed Billy into ours.

At first, I tried to get Billy to talk about the suspects, but he wouldn't say a word. So as he whistled as he worked, I went over everything in my mind. The trouble was almost everyone was still at the top of my list. They can't *all* be the murderer. Wait a minute. Maybe all of them had business interests in the Fenton company.

The three of us finished the last of the boxes Billy had brought home, and we all went to bed. As I lay there unable to sleep, I realized I had to consider the possibility that the whole council participated in the murder. What was that book of Agatha Christie's that I read? I'll think of it in the morning. The end turned out to be they *all* did it. If *everyone* is still at the top of my list, maybe there's a reason for it. With that thought in mind, I fell asleep.

CHAPTER TWENTY-EIGHT

A BLANKET OF snow covered the ground when I let Bingo out in the morning, and the white stuff was still falling down, softly but steadily. Bingo ran around outside like a mad dog, snapping at the falling white flakes and kicking up his heels. Billy beckoned me back to bed for a quick cuddle. And I do mean quick, because he always left the house before me and Aiden.

Five minutes later, Bingo scratched at the door to come in. Snow covered his back and face, so Billy jumped up to retrieve a towel from the bathroom. After I dried Bingo off, I got dressed, woke Aiden, and began preparing breakfast, just as Billy filled his thermos with hot coffee and ran out the door.

Aiden ate his usual cereal and juice with pulp. I had offered him eggs or oatmeal dozens of times, and he always refused. Although I wouldn't let him eat the sugary cereals, he seemed to gravitate toward the more healthy ones, anyway. The only different breakfast he had was on Sundays when we all ate pancakes. Today I had oatmeal. I usually switched off between oatmeal and eggs, though once in a while I would have cereal along with Aiden.

We got dressed, got ready to leave, packed everything up, and ran to the car. Snow was still falling down, though lighter than before. Without even asking Aiden if he wanted me to drive him to school, I parked in the back of the historical society, and Aiden and I got out of the car. Bingo would stay inside until I returned.

Knowing Aiden *always* wanted to walk to school in the snow, I had worn my snow boots and somehow forgotten my heels at home. They were important to me, but right then, I thought about the trek to school in the wet snow. It didn't snow often in the mountains of Arizona, but when it did, we always walked. Aiden loved it so much that I started enjoying the walk, too, so it was no hardship for me.

When we arrived at school, I kissed him goodbye, waved to Pamela the principal, who stood outside snow or shine greeting the kids and their parents, and I walked as fast as my fat little legs could carry me back to my car. I let Bingo out, hurried into the historical society, brushed the snow off my coat, and stamped my feet to get the snow off my boots. Maybe later I would return home to get my heels. Right now, though, the snow boots were perfect.

Petra was already sitting at her desk, studying. That wasn't unusual, but I took a double take. She wore the same clothes as yesterday. "Hi, Petra," I said, trying to sound nonchalant. Petra dressed weird, but she had never done *that* before.

"Don't even say it, Lorry. I worked late, fell asleep at my desk, end of story." All that without even turning toward me. Then she added, "End. From the old English, finish, destroy, die. So let it die and leave me alone."

When she stole a glance at me, I noticed her cheeks were still tear-stained. The tracks looked fresh. I walked to my office thinking there was more going on than her sleeping at her desk. Why would she not sleep at home if *all that happened* was that she broke up with Mason? Well, I don't mean *all* in the sense that it's minor. She *is* a teenager, and breakups happen. A tragedy, but not catastrophic. At least it shouldn't be. Though living it would be difficult. Feeling more compassion after I thought about it, I turned around to comfort her.

"No, Lorry, I don't need anything from you right now. Just go back to work and leave me alone."

Sometimes Petra scared me. Right now, I felt really bad for her. Poor Petra. Her father was a useless drunk, and from the little I knew of her mother, she wasn't the touchy-feely type. Petra had no one. Wait, Zack came in yesterday to hug her. At least she had him. And Zack was a good guy. I should call him to come see her again. That would be a kind thing to do, and Petra needed kind right now. But I checked my email, got caught up in some cute animal forwards, and forgot what I had planned to do.

When I finished going through my email, I looked out the window and the snow had stopped, leaving behind a bright blue and white day. It was beautiful, although it would have been more beautiful out at the ranch and out of town. That thought made me smile. It was the first time I had thought about the ranch in a homey kind of way. Fondly. It made me realize how much I loved the place already. The wide spacious surroundings, the beautiful house and furniture, and especially the horses. It was perfect for us! I knew it!

The only bad feeling I had about it was Charlie. So-called Uncle Charlie who probably wasn't anybody's uncle. Why would Billy want him around, anyway? Just because he *came* with the house, didn't mean we had to *keep* him, did it? My new personal project was to think of a way to get rid of him—I don't mean kill him—but there were other ways.

I forced myself to think happier thoughts about the house. After Martha moved out and we moved in, we would have to have a house warming party! It would be wonderful. And my birthday was coming up, so we could do both at once. No gifts, of course.

I was used to that, though. When I was a little girl and had birthday parties for all my little friends, my mother always wrote on the invitation "No gifts please." She always said it was because we were rich and needed nothing, which made a certain amount of sense. What made me feel bad, though, is the other little rich kids in town had birthday parties, and their mothers never wrote anything like that. It was like I wasn't good enough or something. Bad memory. Get yourself back to happy thoughts of the house. I'd try.

Then I looked at my watch and came to my senses. It was getting later every minute. If I hurried next door, maybe I could catch Paul Gallagher. Kasey said he sometimes came in the mornings before school. Jumping up and grabbing my purse, I told Bingo to stay and then slid outside and sloshed through the snowy sidewalk to the Kafe.

CHAPTER TWENTY-NINE

AS I OPENED the door to the Kafe, I realized I hadn't told Petra I was leaving. She probably didn't want to know, anyway, and nobody would come to the historical society to visit in this weather.

When I walked in, Kasey was behind the counter and raised her head up to get my attention. She shifted her eyes to the left side, and I saw Paul Gallagher sitting there waiting for his order. Kasey winked at me without smiling, and I took it to mean she would try to delay him so I could ask him some questions.

I sidled up to him trying to look nonchalant and then plunked my fat butt into the chair next to his. "Hello, Paul." My mouth was open to introduce myself, when he looked at me.

"Hello, Lorry."

"Oh! Hi!"

"We met at one of Kasey and John's parties. You know, besides the other night."

The other night was the council meeting. And since Paul and Kasey's husband John worked together, that would make sense. Nodding my head, I said, "Yes, I remember," though I really didn't.

He tapped some coins on the table trying to get Kasey's attention, but she ignored him, bless her. "So who do you think did it, Paul? You know, the murder."

Paul looked at me in a serious way. "I don't know. But I definitely don't think Martha did it. That whole idea is ridiculous." He tapped the coins on the counter again and looked in Kasey's direction.

"Um, where were you when it happened?"

He smiled as if he caught me at something. "I was at the front looking at the bulletin board."

Someone else had said that, so there was only one other thing to ask. "Was anyone else there with you?"

Paul nodded. "Yes, there was. Elizabeth Conroy. I guess that means I have an alibi," he said without any sign of guile.

"Either that or you two were in on it together."

After pounding on the counter with the coins, he looked over at Kasey and said, "Hey, Kasey. What's the holdup today?" Pointing to his watch, he said, "Come on! I'll be even later than I already am."

"It's your meeting day today, Paul, and I know how much you hate that. So I'm doing you a favor!" She smiled at him and sashayed away.

Paul turned toward me. "Look, Elizabeth is the one who talked me into trying out for the council. And I *hate* it! I can't wait to get off, and as soon as they settle this thing, I plan to quit."

"Why not quit now?" I asked.

"Now *that* would make me look guilty! It's perfectly logical. The one who gets out the earliest is the one who did it," he said, as Kasey brought him his coffee. Picking it up, he waved as he walked past and out the door.

"Thanks, Kasey," I said.

"Don't you even want a coffee?" she asked.

"Sure. And a croissant." Might as well go for it.

I paid her, gave her a big tip worth more than the coffee and croissant, and returned to the historical society.

I walked in to Bingo wagging his tail madly like I had disappeared for hours. Dogs are like that. They make you feel appreciated. Petra, meanwhile, talked excitedly on the phone. It felt good to hear her animated again. Her melancholy attitude of the last couple of days had worried me. After putting the coffee and croissant on my desk, I popped my head back to her office to wave to her and let her know I was back.

What I saw shocked me and scared me even more. While Petra still talked in an excited manner, tears ran down her face. And they didn't look like happy tears. Pretending I didn't notice, I returned to my office and sipped my coffee wondering what was going on.

I didn't have to wonder long. When she got off the phone, she came to the place between our offices and stood there. "Guess what?" she said. "My aunt in Denver sent my mom a bus ticket to visit her. Mom is thrilled, but worried Dad will be mad. She has to leave today, and he's passed out, so she can't even tell him, and she knows better than to wake him up. I told her to leave him a note."

"Does she need a ride to the bus?" I asked.

"No. My aunt sent her money for a taxi, too. Mom doesn't know what's going on, but she's happy about it."

That seemed to be my opening, so I jumped right in. "So why aren't *you* happy about it?"

Petra shook her head. "Oh, Lorry. Quit." She walked back to her office. When she got there, she said, "She was packing as we talked, and the taxi arrived before we got off the phone. She's already on her way to Coyote Moon to catch the bus. It all happened so quick."

Then I heard her clicking away at her keyboard, so I said nothing more.

CHAPTER THIRTY

I SAT AT my desk thinking. Getting motivated to work felt difficult with everything still so unsettled. So I thought about the murder and my list of suspects. Almost everybody made it to my list of suspects! But I still had more to go. Douglas Gates was the only person on the council I hadn't talked to yet. Off the council, I still needed to talk to Russ Tabor and the son of the deceased, Todd Fenton. The son stayed a viable suspect, especially because he kept thinking that *I* did it! And Russ Tabor just felt suspicious to me.

Before I made an effort to see any of those three people, I thought a trip to the scene of the crime might be a good idea. If I could get a good idea of where everyone was, it might help figuring out where they weren't—murdering Christopher Fenton.

The Arizona sun had melted most of the snow off the roads, but—at least the one in front of the historical society—still appeared slushy, so it surprised me when I heard a motorcycle pull up in front and park. And it surprised me more to see that it was Mason. So much for my assumption that he and Petra broke up.

He burst into the door without even stamping his feet and walked straight past me to Petra's office.

"Hello, Mason," I said as I felt the breeze when he passed.

"Lorry," he said without stopping.

Next thing I knew Petra was crying, and Mason was crooning, "I'm sorry. I'm so sorry. Petra, I'm sorry."

What was he sorry about? Had he screwed around on her or something? My mind always went there because that was my first husband's favorite trick. But I'm not going there. Where I was going was to the Town Offices to look around. And then the phone rang.

"Rutledge Historical Soc—oh, hi, Billy . . . Do what? . . . How'd that happen? . . . Won't I get stuck, too? . . . All right. I'll leave right now. . . . Love you, too. . . . Bye."

Billy wanted me to go to the new house and pick up Hugo on the way. Poor Hugo had tried to drive through the snow in his Cadillac and had gotten stuck. Billy assured me that my all-wheel drive Rav4 would not get stuck. So I packed up everything I needed, which wasn't much, and walked past Petra and Mason standing up by her desk and hugging. Petra stood there still crying and Mason comforted her by rubbing his hand over her back. Since Mason had everything under control, I walked by without saying a word.

When I got to the back door, I stooped down to pick up Bingo. No sense in his feet getting all dirty and then jumping into my car. I stepped out the door and saw Christa leaning against her car, smoking. She waved, grinned at me, and held up her half-smoked cigarette. "Still trying to quit!" Then she dropped it, smashed it into the ground, and got into her car.

I had to give her credit for trying, even though it didn't look like she was succeeding. Now that I knew her better, I'd have to check out her shop. Maybe it wasn't as juvenile as I had assumed. And you don't need to remind me about assume. I know all about what it does to "u" and "me."

Opening the door of my car, I opened my arms and let Bingo jump in. He moved over to the passenger seat like a regular person. What a smart boy! Then I slid in beside him and started the car.

We buzzed down the slushy alley and made a left on Bridge Street and another left on High. I hoped Billy was right about me not getting stuck on the road. With all the snow melting, it seemed like a real possibility. It didn't surprise me that Hugo's Cadillac got stuck.

We drove past the barrier and onto the dirt road. Billy was right; my Rav4 drove through it with no problem at all. Less than fifteen minutes later, we came upon Hugo's Cadillac off to the side of the road. The back tire was deep in the mud. It looked like he had tried to gun the engine to get it unstuck, which only got him more stuck.

I pulled up beside him figuring he would see me and jump in the car. That didn't happen. He didn't see me. His head rested on the steering wheel. I would have thought he had hurt himself except for two things. One, Billy had said nothing about an injury. And two, I could see his shoulders were shaking. Poor Hugo looked like he was crying.

I didn't know what to do. If I honked, it might scare him and make him feel even worse than he already did. If I got out of the car and knocked on the window, he would know that I knew he was crying. What a dilemma. Before too much longer, Bingo stood up on his hind legs and looked out the window. When he recognized who it was, he barked. I don't know how Hugo heard him with both windows—his and mine—closed, but he looked up, and that's all it took. He smiled a half smile, slid out his door, locked his car, and stepped into mine.

He looked at me unashamedly, not even trying to hide the tear stains on his cheeks. "Thank you for doing this, Lorry. I'm afraid I got myself into more trouble than I had anticipated."

"No problem, Hugo. For you, the world!" Then I patted him on the hand.

Tears started rolling down his face, and Bingo jumped up to lick them off. Hugo let him.

"I miss her so much."

Before I could engage my mouth filter, I said, "She just left yesterday."

Hugo nodded. "I know. But we've never spent even one night apart. That was the first time. I don't know what I'll do without her tonight. Last night, I stayed up the whole night pacing and worrying about her."

As if in answer to his silent prayer, his phone rang. Not even looking at who the caller was, he pressed the button and said eagerly, "Martha? . . . Oh," he said, disappointment apparent in his voice, "Hi, Mason."

Mason? I wondered. Why would Mason be calling Hugo? I only needed to listen to find out the answer to that question.

"Yes, sure she can stay, as long as she wants. I only have the one couple that will be here two more nights. I've cancelled everyone else. I tried to cancel them, but— . . . oh, okay. . . . she could? That would be wonderful, Mason! I would appreciate that so much! Wow! Truly an answer to my prayers."

I think I just said that. Or thought it, anyway. This conversation got more and more interesting.

Hugo continued, "She's welcome to go there anytime. The key is under the mat in the front. Her room will be at the top of the stairs and then right to the one with the bathroom. . . . Yes, I think it's awesome, too . . . You're welcome, and Mason, thank *you*! Bye."

He turned toward me, the tears dried and his face ear to ear with a big smile. "Petra is going to stay at our bed and breakfast and take care of the guests, so I can stay with Martha. I'm so happy!"

"Hugo, that's great! Do you know why Petra is staying there and not at her own house?" Inquiring minds wanted to know.

But he ignored me. I don't think it was deliberate—his mind was on a different track.

"No more nights apart!" He clapped his hands. "Martha and me," he sang, "happy as can be! K-I-S-S-I-N-G."

"Very cute, Hugo." This was getting a little too mushy for me. It was bad enough having to watch Petra and Mason kiss, but Hugo and Martha? Kill me now!

"I've been a bloody wreck, but Martha has been fine." He put his hand briefly on my shoulder. "By the way, Lorry, bloody is a

British expression. The couple we have staying with us now are British, and they use it all the time. I kind of like it."

It made me happy the way everything had worked out for Martha and Hugo. I didn't like Martha having to stay there alone with that Charlie man.

"In fact," Hugo continued, "maybe Martha is having *too* good of a time. She told me all about Charlie and what a good time they're having together. I told her I was worried that she'd leave me for a younger man." He chuckled.

His laugh was good to hear, but two things about that comment bothered me. Could I be that wrong about Charlie? Martha liked him? Well, that wasn't strange, because Martha liked everybody. That's the way Martha was. She would like a serial killer if she got to know one. So, no, I'm not going to take Martha's fondness for Charlie as a reason to stop disliking him. I'd need a better reason than that.

The other thing that bothered me was Hugo said Charlie was a *younger* man. Younger? I thought he was the same age or *older* than Hugo and Martha! Maybe it was being out in the sun or smoking or drinking that caused him to look like that. Ah, well. Color me humbled—but I still didn't like him.

By this time, Hugo was looking around enjoying himself. Now he looked at me with concern showing on his face. "How much farther? If I had known the ranch was this far out, I would have been even more worried about her."

"The only ones who know where she is are me and Billy and Wichita. No one else has a clue. So she's safe."

"All the same, I'm glad Charlie is with her."

Indeed. "I don't think I've passed the turnoff," I said looking around me at the road.

"I haven't seen a left turnoff since you picked me up, so I don't think so."

And like magic, the turnoff appeared. Just like downtown. But not downtown. Oh, you know what I mean.

I turned onto Sylvan Way and a minute later drove through the entrance to the ranch and pulled into the driveway.

The front door opened and Martha stepped out, her hands on her cheeks and tears streaming from her eyes. Hugo opened the door, and before I had a chance to tell him to be careful because of the ice, he had jumped out of the car and into her arms.

There was no ice. Someone had cleared all the snow off the driveway and the walkway in front of the house. I didn't think Martha would have done that. Snow could be heavy work. Could it have been Charlie?

CHAPTER THIRTY-ONE

AFTER WAVING GOODBYE to the lovebirds, I began the long trek back to the historical society. As much as I wanted to go over my suspect list, I felt I had to give some thought to what just happened. Hugo and Martha, separated for one day, acted like they had been apart for months. It was like when you left a dog for a few minutes, and when you return, the dog acts like you've been gone for ages. Bingo does that.

I hoped Billy and I would still be that much in love in forty years. For my part, I knew I would love him until the end, but for his part, I wasn't so sure. Because you *never know*. And that fear, if you want to call it that, had nothing to do with Billy but had to do with me. Billy had never given me any reason to doubt his love or the duration of his love. Eddie had loved me once, too. At least I think he did—unless he was just with me because of my money—or rather my mother's money. And that was a distinct possibility. So if Eddie never really loved me, it made me feel a lot better about Billy never stopping loving me—if that makes any sense. It does to me.

The other thought banging around in my head was Charlie shoveling the snow for Martha. No one else could have done it. And I didn't think it was Charlie's job. He didn't really have a job; his only responsibility was taking care of the horses if Billy wasn't around to do it. Horses and snow were two separate things. He had no reason to do that except, dare I say it, being nice.

Before I get too carried away with accolades for Charlie, let me reconsider. There were good guys who did bad things. Just like there were bad guys who did good things. Example: a serial killer who treated his mother well. So the only logical explanation—and I try to be logical, though I don't often succeed—was that Charlie was a downright disagreeable old guy who could do good things. That didn't mean he would do them all the time, but occasionally, he *could* do them.

After going back and forth over all these thoughts and wondering if I was right or wrong, or maybe even both, I arrived back at the historical society. As I drove by the front, I didn't see Mason's motorcycle. Good. I wouldn't feel as weird going inside if Mason had left. Petra was a whole 'nother story. What was going on with her? I had no idea and couldn't even make a wild guess. Looking back, I guess I should have known. But how could I?

Parking in the back, I picked Bingo up again and unlocked the back door to the society. Instead of saying anything, I walked quietly up to the front. With all this weirdness going on, I felt like I was walking on eggshells around Petra, and believe me, that wasn't a good feeling. It used to be a way of life for me. And it wasn't a good feeling at all.

When I walked past Petra's desk, she wasn't there. She must have gone off with Mason somewhere. I couldn't blame her for that, as I had been gone most of the morning myself. Moving toward the front door to change the closed sign to open, I realized Petra hadn't bothered—or remembered—to flip the sign when she left. At least she had locked the door. Opening it and gazing outside, I saw that the only footprints in the melting snow were my own big-booted ones, and two other sets leading to the street where Mason had parked his motorcycle. And the only track in the street was from Mason's motorcycle.

So it didn't matter that she didn't flip the sign. Not that it would anyway, if the place was closing down and turning into a mall. I hoped that wouldn't happen. And that reminded me to call Bryan again to see if he had made any progress with the project I had given him.

Sitting down at my desk, I checked my email, and found nothing of any interest. I didn't feel like going upstairs and doing more scanning. What I really felt like doing was going over the suspect list for the murder. I should write it all down instead of trying to keep it in my teensy-weensy brain. Isn't that how it works? Big butt, small brain. No, I guess what it really means is cold hands warm heart. I felt my hands, but it's difficult to tell if your own hands are cold. Go ahead. Try it. I dare you.

I opened the center drawer to my desk—which was full to overflowing with stuff I needed to sift through, throw out, or organize—and grabbed the nearest pen. Then I opened the middle drawer on the left side to pull out a pad of paper. Ready to start, I sat there staring at the empty page. Where should I begin? Who popped out as the top of my suspect list? Who was at the bottom? Everyone was at the top, because I hadn't eliminated anyone yet! So I started in alphabetical order, using first names.

Anthony Petrelli. Sad to say, I had ruined any chance of finding out if he had an alibi, but I knew one thing for sure. Anyone who is that vehement that someone else had done the murder was trying to deflect guilt from himself. And that goes double for anyone who thought Martha could commit murder.

Brent Lindsay. He had a point in his favor for not attending the meeting that was to condemn and fire Martha. And he got another point for calling what they had planned to do to Martha "dirty work." And I appreciated a man who calls 'em like he sees 'em, because I'm like that.

The strike—and it felt like a big strike—against him was how he ended the conversation. His body language, the way he walked away, and saying so flatly that he didn't know who did it, but he knew it wasn't him. It had an air of guilt associated with it. Not that I knew anything about body language, but I'm a good guesser. I think I am, anyway.

Christa Hawthorne. She could be at the bottom of the list because she voted *for* the sale, and like Brent Lindsay, she had not attended the meeting to oust Martha from her job. The main thing about Christa—I know this is silly—but how comfortable she looked with a gun in her hands. Granted, it was all in my imagination, and granted that Elizabeth looked almost as comfortable. Still, I couldn't bring myself to eliminate Christa off the suspect list. So she would stay. Also, she had told Billy she was in the bathroom but hadn't seen Martha. That was peculiar. Maybe even more so because Russell Tabor said he saw her coming out of the bathroom which verified her alibi. Keep her on! Take her off! Keep her on! It was all so confusing.

A needle of doubt shot through me. What if Martha lied about being in the bathroom? I had never considered that before. In all the time I'd known her, she had never told one lie. But I've known her less than a year. And if someone tells a lie and you don't find out it's a lie, then how would you know? I shook my head. No. I refused to go there. I still believed in the truth of Martha's words and her complete and total innocence. Yes, for sure. I believed Martha.

That brings us to Elizabeth Conroy. Oh, no, wait, I'm skipping Douglas Gates. Shoot. That made sense, though, since I knew nothing about him. I needed to go see him soon. Kasey said he was a drinker. That should make him easy enough to find— check the bars.

Now for Elizabeth Conroy. I knew Billy didn't think she did it —not from anything he said, but from the sound of his voice when he talked to her at the secret council meeting. She said Billy had proven no one innocent, yet, including Martha. And she said Martha had a motive and could have done the killing, and she even had me considering it! Imagine!

Elizabeth was convincing. No wonder she had been principal of the high school for so long. She said the murderer could be anyone—including her. Maybe she was telling the truth. Maybe it *was* her. There was the vision of her with the gun in her hand

and looking pleased. Although that didn't strike me so much as including herself in who the murderer could be.

Joe Stoddard, the mayor, doesn't count because he was with me when the murder occurred. I can count him out for sure. I think.

Paul Gallagher was a conundrum for me. My gut feeling was that he didn't do it. He had said he was at the bulletin board with Elizabeth. Yet Elizabeth never mentioned seeing Paul there, although she said she was there. And him saying he planned to quit the High Council as soon as Billy solved the murder, because if he quit before that it would make him look guilty. Anyone afraid of looking guilty might be guilty. He stayed on the list.

And last but not—well, you know what I was going to say— was Russ Tabor. I knew nothing about him. Petra had said he was the town clerk, so he must work under Martha. Or at least *did*. I wondered if he'd be elevated to the town manager until Martha returned. Why would I need to see the town clerk? I think he has something to do with the town records. I'm sure I could come up with some reason to look something up.

As I was about to put the list away, I remembered something important. Todd Fenton. He wasn't on the council, but like Russ Tabor, he was most definitely a viable suspect. I didn't know where to find him, and I didn't know why he would want to stop the sale of the historical society, but—wait.

Maybe he didn't want to stop it and instead wanted it all to himself. He was the son, after all. Didn't he stand to inherit everything? I'd have to find out if there were any other siblings who would profit from the father's death. Maybe the killer could be one of them, or Todd was in it with a sibling. The possibilities were endless.

In the meantime, *everyone* was on my list and *no one* was off it. I'd have to figure something out to narrow it down. Maybe Billy would share some details with me. Then again, maybe he wouldn't. He doesn't like me getting involved in finding murderers, and somehow I always do. Get involved, that is. Although I find them, too. And it usually gets me in trouble—the scary kind.

CHAPTER THIRTY-TWO

I SWIVELED MY chair to face the fish tank behind me. It had been a while since my life was in such upheaval that I needed the tranquility of the fish to calm me. And although it wasn't in upheaval now, I thought the meditative quality of their movements would allow me to figure everything out easier. But after my first glance at the fish, I heard a rumbling noise coming from outside.

Turning back toward the window, I saw Petra swinging her leg off the back of Mason's motorcycle. I thought she would give him a quick peck on the lips and come inside, or maybe a long passionate kiss. Who knows with Petra and Mason? Instead, what happened was Mason got off the motorcycle, set the kickstand, and gave her a hug. A long, tight, comforting hug. Petra clung to him for several minutes as Mason rubbed her back. Then he pulled away, gave her a quick kiss, climbed back on his motorcycle and sped off, with Petra watching. Standing up and leaning over my desk, I could see Mason drive down High Street, turn on Bridge Street, and go over the bridge toward Coyote Moon.

When Petra came through the front door, I had already arranged myself to be looking at the fish tank, so she wouldn't think I was spying on her—which of course I was. But she needn't know that. When she came in, I turned toward her and said, "Oh, hi Petra. Isn't Mason coming in?" That was an innocent question, wasn't it? I hoped so.

"No, he has to go back to Flag. He's got classes this afternoon."

"Oh, I thought you guys had broken up."

Petra looked at me and shook her head, looking thoughtful. "No, Lorry," she breathed a deep breath out, "That's not what it was."

"Oh," I said, with an upward lilt as if it was a question.

"No, it's, it's—" said Petra.

This was it. She was going to tell me what was going on. I held my breath and didn't say a word. Give her space. Let her tell me of her own accord. Wait for it.

Then the phone rang, and the moment was gone. Dead and gone. "Rutledge Historical Society. . . . Yes, we're open today. . . . I don't know about tomorrow. With the pending sale, every day is a new day. . . . Five o'clock today. Like I said, I'm not sure about tomorrow. . . . Yes, well, I would suggest calling tomorrow before you come. . . . Yes, you're welcome. Goodbye!" What a waste of an important moment.

When I turned back to where Petra had been standing, she had disappeared, and I heard the computer keys in her office clicking away. The moment had gone, and it wasn't my place to ask her what was going on. Huffing silently to myself for the lost moment, I signed off on my computer, patted my leg for Bingo, and stood up and walked toward Petra's desk. "I don't think anyone's coming today, so I'm going to go run another errand. Unless, you know—"

I hoped the comment would spur her on to tell me what she was about to tell me before, but she didn't even turn toward me, just kept typing. "That's fine. I'll see you when I see you."

After loading Bingo into my car, I drove the short distance to the Rutledge Town Offices where the murder took place. I had no idea what I'd find there, but I felt like I needed to go. Looking carefully and with an objective eye at the murder scene was always a good idea. Why didn't I always do it? Now that I *was* doing it, it made perfect sense that I should. So there.

As I pulled out from the back of the historical society, I had a funny feeling that I couldn't identify. It felt like *danger*. What was that about? *Danger?* At the town offices? That made no sense at all. Granted a murder had occurred, but still. I felt fine about ignoring that feeling, because it was ridiculous.

We parked in the back parking lot of the Town Office, and because there *was* no front parking lot. Leaning over, I left my purse in the shadows of the front seat. Holding my car keys in my hand, I left Bingo in the car and walked the short walkway toward the modern pink and gray concrete building. I pulled open the glass door with the gold lettering, *Rutledge Town Offices*, and paused for a moment in the waiting area. That's where the bulletin board where Elizabeth Conroy and Paul Gallagher said they were standing when someone shot old man Fenton. It was a small room. Had anyone else been there, he or she would have been noticed.

I walked through the interior door and stood there, considering my options. Straight ahead behind a glassed-in area, sat the receptionist faced the other direction talking to someone. That wasn't one of my options. I didn't want to announce myself, anyway. To the left, down the hallway, was Martha's office. Or should I say Martha's *old* office? To the right, down that hallway was the emergency doorway—which did not have an alarm— and a couple of other offices, including the mayor's. I'd start down that way.

The office doors were closed. I didn't know if the mayor was in or not, though it didn't matter. He wasn't someone I needed to see. He couldn't have been the murderer. I wondered where Russ Tabor's office was. If I could talk to him, it would either shoot him up to the top of my list or take him off completely. There was a door that said *Town Clerk*, but it was closed, too. No matter. I marched my butt up to the emergency door and, holding it open with my foot, stepped outside. This was where the murder had been committed. Right here, almost where I stood, someone had shot Christopher Fenton dead.

CHAPTER THIRTY-THREE

I STOOD OUT there with my foot in the door and looked around. There was a small cement area, just big enough for a couple of people to stand and smoke. I ascertained that because there were cigarette butts all over the ground. As I looked at how disgusting they looked lying there, I noticed a big rock lying next to the door. It looked like people used it to prop the door open so they wouldn't have to leave their foot in the door like I was doing. I was going to pick the rock up and put it in the door, but then wondered if Billy had fingerprinted it. I didn't know if you could take fingerprints off a rock, but maybe there was a smooth surface on it. Leaving my foot where it was, I gazed around at— nothing. Besides the cigarette butts, the rock, and the cement, there was nothing out here. Except the tape on the ground outlining the body of the deceased.

Stepping inside the door, I let it close behind me with a re- sounding whoosh. Walking back down the hallway, all the office doors remained closed. Where was everybody? The receptionist behind the glass was still talking, though this time it was on the phone. She didn't even look up when I passed. I moved down the other hallway toward the meeting room and Martha's office. Voices floated out at me from Martha's office, so I stopped out- side the door and peered in.

The mayor sat behind the desk, looking all pomp and circum- stance, and basking in his own importance. When he saw me, he stood up, narrowed his eyes, and said, "Miss Lockharte, *what* are you doing here?"

All right, if that's how he was going to play it, I could handle it. "It's Ms."

He shook his head and shrugged his shoulders. "What?"

"It's Ms. Miss indicates a single woman, and I am a married woman. So it's Ms. Lockharte, not Miss Lockharte," I began. Putting my hands on my hips, I continued, "What am I doing here? Perhaps I was under the mistaken impression that this was a *public* building. Unless you've taken it on your own to sell this building to the highest bidder."

The mayor blushed a bright, blood red and said nothing. I sometimes had that effect on people, and I was proud of it. This time, though, it looked like the mayor was about to blow a gasket, and it scared me.

Since I didn't want to stare at him, because it might make him blow that much sooner, I looked at the two men sitting in front of *Martha's* desk. One was Todd Fenton, dressed in a dark blue and yellow striped sweatsuit, like he was out jogging and just stopped by to see what the mayor was selling today. The other man was Russ Tabor who had mostly gray receding hair that looked greasy. He wore a dress shirt with a tie loosely knotted at his neck. He had a scowl on his face, but I got the feeling that he always did.

While the mayor tried to regain his cool, Todd Fenton spoke up. "Ah, so it's the town murderess. Have you come back to see if you left any clues behind at the scene of the crime?"

The mayor came back to earth, then. "She was with me, Todd. I can guarantee you that it wasn't her."

Now it was time for me to point out what I thought of Todd's attitude. "*You* seem awfully flippant for a man who lost his father a few days ago. What are *you* doing back at the scene of the crime? Or more importantly, where were *you* when your father was murdered? Hiding the gun in the bushes, maybe?" Although I didn't remember any bushes outside when I looked around, it seemed like a good thing to say at the time.

Todd became almost as red as the mayor. "I had been talking to my father outside. I stepped inside to use the men's room, and we planned to meet back in the conference room. He never showed up. You know the rest."

"Was anyone in the bathroom with you to verify your presence?"

"Enough of this!" said the mayor in an elevated voice.

"So no alibi, huh Todd?" I pressed.

"All right, all right, enough of these accusations. We know who did it, and what's done is done." The mayor gathered up papers from the desk, straightened them, and put them back down again, while I stood there slack-jawed. "I was in here showing Russ his new job of town manager."

"Whoa, wait a minute, whoa there," I said—because now that we owned a ranch, I was getting into the whole cowboy-western theme. I held my left hand in front of my chest so the fingers were vertical and pointed at the ceiling, and held my right hand horizontal on top of the left, in a time-out football motion. I couldn't think of any western way to do that.

"First, you said that we know who did it." I walked over to the mayor, then bent over with my big butt in the air and got right in his face. "You couldn't possibly mean Martha, because I'm married to the sheriff, and last I heard—this morning as a matter of fact—he had not yet discovered *who* did it. And you mean showing Russ his new *temporary* job, right Mayor? Because Martha is still a member of the team here and is on *vacation*." I stood up and crossed my arms, looking down at him. "Isn't that right, Mayor?"

Then I fixed my gaze on Russ Tabor. "And you, looking like someone just stepped on your foot." Russ's face twitched. "Where were *you* when Mr. Fenton was murdered? That murder was your lucky day, wasn't it? New job, promotion. Maybe the killing had nothing to do with the sale of the historical society. You wanted everyone to believe that and overlook who really did it. In the bathroom my foot! I think it was *you*!" At this I pointed my right hand, finger outstretched—index finger, not the middle one—"it was you, wasn't it! Confess now, Russ. It's good for the soul!"

The outburst shocked everyone, including me. It poured out of me, unplanned, unsolicited, suddenly it was just there.

"I think it's time for you to leave, Ms. Lockharte. Get out of my office, now," the mayor said.

Although he didn't say it angrily, he said it in a way that made it hard not to listen. I walked toward the door, stepped out, and then popped my head back in. "It's *Martha's* office!" Then and only then did I walk out of the town office building with my head held high.

Color me haughty! I strolled out to the car so happy that I got the last word with that arrogant mayor. Until I got to the car, that is. I reached for my purse, and that's when I realized that I had locked the purse in the car and had been holding the keys in my hand. Looking in my hand as if for verification, I saw nothing. Palm to face. I knew I hadn't left them outside when I went out that emergency door. There was only one place I could have left them. When I leaned forward to get in the mayor's face, I must have inadvertently set them down.

Scratch the haughty. Color me contrite. Now I had to go back in to his—I mean *Martha's*—office and retrieve my keys. There were no other alternatives. Well, there were, but they were unpalatable. I could leave the car in the parking lot, walk over to the sheriff's station, hope Billy was there, and get the extra key from him. But he might not be there, and it would be worse if he was, because he'd know that I'd been poking around. No, there was only one solution. Put on my happy face and go back in there and get my keys.

Walking back into the town office building, my head wasn't held as high. But after walking through the exterior door, I held it higher, because I wanted to return with at least some of my dignity intact. The mayor was handing Russ Tabor a clipboard when I walked in. "Excuse me, gentlemen," I said and picked up my keys. "I think these are mine." As I was about to turn and leave, I heard it. We all heard it. A gunshot. Two more in rapid succession.

"Billy!" I shouted. Then I turned and ran for my car.

CHAPTER THIRTY-FOUR

I DON'T KNOW how I knew those bullets had been aimed at Billy, but I think it must have been that weird feeling of danger when I left the historical society. Bingo was barking like a mad dog when I scooted myself inside the car, so I could only surmise that he knew something was amiss, too. Sitting in the car, I grabbed for my purse so I could call Billy. Wait. If he was in the middle of a gun battle—though I had heard no bullets since the first three—I didn't want to distract him. What could I do?

Having made my decision, I put my purse back on the floor, started the car, and headed toward the Sheriff's Station down the street. I pulled into the parking lot, but Billy's car wasn't there. Still, they would know what was happening. After patting Bingo on the head, I jumped out of the car and raced to the door, as fast as my three-inch heeled feet could carry me. By the time I used both hands to open the heavy front door, I was out of breath when I arrived at the receptionist.

"Is Billy okay?" I gasped.

"He called for backup five minutes ago," Vanessa said. "Nick raced out of here, and I've heard nothing since." She looked concerned.

"I'm worried, Vanessa."

"I know, Lorry. So am I. But I'm hoping no news is good news. And I haven't heard another shot since Billy called for backup. That has to be good," she said with a slight smile.

Vanessa looked worried, not just because it was her job, but because Nick, the cop that Billy called for backup, was her older brother. She was the receptionist and "Civilian Officer" with the kind face whom I met when I first came in this place to get fingerprinted. Don't ask. It was another one of those experiences that I'd rather forget. Although not half as bad as when I was locked in the holding cell. Definitely don't ask about that.

"I don't know what to do," I said, on the verge of tears. "When I heard those shots, I knew they were aimed at Billy."

"Like I said, Lorry, there hasn't been another shot since he called for help."

I felt a stab of hope. "Oh, so Nick never called in and said, 'officer down!' or anything like that? That's a good thing, isn't it?"

She stood up and squeezed my arm. "Nobody ever called in with an officer down, so I'm sure Billy is fine. I'd say 'don't worry about it,' but I know you will, so I won't even say it!" That made us both laugh. "Do you want to come back here and wait, Lorry? You're welcome to."

It was a restricted area for sheriff's department employees, but since I was the sheriff's wife, Vanessa could afford to be amiable. And I was about to accept when the door burst open and Billy strode in.

"Lorry!" He took two big steps forward and threw his arms around me. "I'm sorry. I'm so sorry."

I had no idea what he was talking about. And as glad as I was to see him, I was afraid to ask and more afraid of the answer. If he was sorry because something had happened to our son, Aiden, I didn't know what I would do. So in my most adult-sounding little girl voice, I said, "Why?"

Billy pulled away from me and put his hands on my shoulders. "Because I know how much you don't want to be a widow. And someone shot at me today! Luckily they missed." His eyes left mine for an instant. "Or mostly missed."

"Okay, what do you mean, 'mostly'?" I put my hands on my hips but didn't see any blood coming out of him or any makeshift bandage on him.

"Oh, just this." He turned around and held up his foot so I could see it. Right at the edge of the boot, a bullet had made a hole in the sole. "It's a nick, but it could have been bad."

"Tell me what happened, please." Because I was so glad nothing had happened to him, I hugged him again.

Billy told his story of being on Commercial Street. He had been driving here and there in town following up on leads, talking to people, doing regular sheriff stuff, and he pulled over and parked. He had stepped out of the truck but leaned back in to get his Smokey Bear hat—Billy loves his Smokey Bear hat—and that's when the shot rang out.

"So my hat saved me!" After taking off his hat, he kissed it and put it back on. Then he continued with his story. The shot had gone over his head and broken the opposite window of the car. Billy pushed himself into the car trying to close the door behind him. That's when the second bullet hit his boot. He said it was a chore squeezing past all the equipment between the seats, but he moved onto his side to do it. By that time the door had closed, and the third bullet hit the door. If the shooter had been closer or had a more powerful gun, the bullet could have gone through the door. Billy had gotten lucky.

"Then I called for Nick, and we looked around, but neither of us found anything and there were no more shots." He hugged me again and looked into my eyes. "So," he hesitated, then continued, "this changes things. He or she has come after me. So me and mine are no longer safe. I'd like you to call Aiden's school, and—"

"You don't think he'll go after Aiden, do you?" That scared me. It was bad enough he was shooting at Billy.

"No, I think it's doubtful. But I must be getting close. So, I'd like you to call Aiden's school, ask him to stay the weekend at Lily's house, and then you and I are going to Coyote Moon."

"On a date?" I asked. That was not like Billy to ignore work for a good time.

Billy laughed, and it broke the tension. While Billy told his story, Nick had come in, gone into the reception area, and hugged his sister. They heard this exchange, and they laughed, too.

"No, not on a date. We're getting you a gun."

I crossed my arms. "I don't want a gun! I don't want to kill anybody!"

Billy put his arms on my shoulders again. He has found this calms me. "Now, Lorry. I don't want you to kill anybody, either. But if somebody comes after *you*, I want you to be able to *stop* them. That's all. Stop them. That's reasonable, isn't it?"

"I guess so." Looking down at myself, I shook my head. "A holster will ruin the line of my clothes."

Billy laughed again. "No holster for you, Lorry. We can get you a concealed carry purse, and you can keep the gun in there until you need it."

"I don't know, Billy." I could imagine some plain, unstylish purse, and I didn't want any part of it.

He took his hands off my shoulders, took a step back, and looked more serious than I'd ever seen him. "I'm not messing around with this, Lorry. Either you get a gun, or you're going on a cruise until the case is over." He waited a beat and then continued, "Alaska or the Caribbean?"

Knowing he had won, I whispered or maybe I should say whimpered, "It's too cold for Alaska. I'll get the gun."

Billy smiled. "Great. Call Aiden and I'll pick you up in an hour."

CHAPTER THIRTY-FIVE

DRIVING BACK TO the historical society, I felt calmer, but the situation still bothered me. For Billy to insist that I get a gun, he must think it necessary. And for Billy to think it's necessary, he must be scared. And for Billy to feel scared—well, it made me scared just thinking about it.

I parked; the sun was out and the snow almost gone, so I let Bingo jump out of the car, and we walked inside the back door and up to the front. "Hi, Petra," I said as I walked by.

"Wait!" she said.

It was the most animated I had seen her in days, so I stopped. "What?" I asked.

"What was all the shooting about?"

"Someone shot at Billy. Now he wants Aiden to stay at Lily's, and he wants to buy me a gun."

"Yuck. You're not going to get one, are you? My father has a gun, and I don't even like having it in the house."

"I have to. He said that I had to either get a gun or go on a cruise."

"Choose the cruise, and I'll go with you! How cool is that! Cruise. From Latin in the seventeenth century, 'to cross, sail to and fro.'" She jumped up and clapped her hands. "C'mon, Lorry, let's sail to and fro! What a blast that will be!"

"No, sorry, Petra. I'm getting the gun. He's buying me a concealed carry purse to go with it—probably some drab, dull, purse that won't go with any of my outfits. I hate the thought of that."

"Well, I'm glad Billy's okay," she said, as she sat down and turned back to her computer.

Bingo and I continued to my office, where I picked up the phone and called the school. I spoke to Pamela and explained what was going on. She had heard the shots and understood completely. A few minutes later, Aiden came on the phone.

"Hi, Sweetie . . . Yes, Daddy's fine . . . Would you mind staying at Lily's house for the weekend? . . . Oh, Sage. All weekend? . . . Sure, I don't see why not. It's okay with his mom and all? . . . Yes, you're right, I shouldn't have asked. Of course, it is. . . . I love you, too, sweetie. See ya in a few. Bye."

"Lorry? Are you going to Coyote Moon to get the gun today? Because you're still wearing those atrocious snow boots, and the sun is out."

Looking down, I exclaimed, "Oh, no! You're right! I forgot all about them! Luckily, I have time to run home for my heels. Billy won't be here for another half hour. I have plenty of time to change." Then I heard large footfalls coming from the hallway.

"Too late," said a booming voice. "Billy came early. Forget the boots and let's get going. I have a long night ahead of me, but I want you to have the gun *now*."

His emphasis on the word *now* scared me even more. "All right," I said reluctantly, forgetting all about the heels.

"Hey, Petra."

"Hey, Billy. I'm glad you didn't get shot."

Billy laughed. "Yeah, thanks. Me, too." He turned and walked toward the back. "C'mon, Lor. Let's take your car."

I sat in the passenger seat without fighting it. When I first got the car, I wouldn't let Billy drive it. But it's been a while, and at least I got to drive it first. And Billy was a good driver. Bingo sat on my lap and panted in my face, and I let him.

Billy pulled out of the alley, turned up Bridge Street and crossed the bridge to Broadway. His knitted brows made him look deep in thought. I didn't want to disturb him. After a while, he was tapping his fingers on the steering wheel and didn't seem so self-absorbed, so I spoke up.

"So what kind of gun are you going to get me? A Colt 45? A 44 Magnum?" The only guns I knew were from the movies.

"No, Lorry, neither of those. And this is not a game. This is serious. I'm concerned and want you to be protected."

"I'm sorry," I said. "I'm really uncomfortable doing this."

"You better get comfortable, Lorry. I'm too busy finishing this case right now, but as soon as I can, you'll take a concealed carry class—either from me or someone else."

"*You* can give it to me? That's cool."

"Sure, I became an instructor several years ago. And get used to this, Lorry, because Aiden needs to know how to use a gun, too."

"Absolutely not. He's only seven. He does not need to know how to use a gun. I wasn't happy with what you've already showed him."

"You mean how to check if a gun is loaded? How to unload a gun? Well, you might be interested to know, smarty-pants," Billy smiled at me briefly, then moved his eyes back to the road, "that he has already used that information in a most positive way."

"What do you mean?" I asked.

"Aiden was at a friend's house, and the friend showed him his father's gun—which happened to be loaded. Aiden handled the situation beautifully. He unloaded the gun and when he got home, he discussed it with me. I called the parents, and it won't happen again."

"He never told me about that."

"Aiden and I agreed that you would worry too much, and it was better if you didn't know."

"I'm not sure I like that." I was about to say that Aiden was my son, but he was Billy's son now, too.

"Would you have worried or not?" asked Billy.

"Definitely worried," I answered.

"See? We were right to keep it from you."

"What are John and Kasey doing with a gun, anyway?"

"Lily wasn't the friend I meant," said Billy.

"Then who?" Aiden hung out with Lily a lot. There was no other friend except the one time he went to—oh, no! Sage's house! And Billy had said, *"his* father's" not *"her* father's.""Oh, no. Don't tell me it was Sage! That's where Aiden is now!" Panicked, I reached for my purse and started digging for my phone.

"Not to worry, Lorry. I told you that I talked to his parents. Both Samantha and Mark. The gun now has a gun lock and is perfectly safe." He patted my knee. "See? Aiden and I made the right decision. You didn't need to know."

"I suppose. I'm still not happy with Aiden learning about guns, though."

"His father's the *sheriff*, Lorry." Billy was talking about himself. "There will *always* be guns in our house. He needs to know." He stopped for a second and then continued. "You know what? Let's not talk about this now. When we get there, you can talk to Martin about when he taught his boy about guns. You'll find what he has to say interesting."

I didn't know where the gun shop was, but I recognized where we were in Coyote Moon. "Turn here!" I said.

CHAPTER THIRTY-SIX

BILLY KNEW ME well enough to know that my request, while maybe not *important*, was at least *significant*. So he put on his turn signal and turned right. A block later we were face to face with Boot Barn.

"I know I need new boots, but why did we have to come now? I want to get you the gun and get back to work."

"Oh, that's right, you do need new boots. But..." I pointed to my snow boots—"I didn't want to wear these *galoshes* in public."

"Those aren't galoshes, they're snow boots. And it snowed today. They're perfectly acceptable."

"Not for me."

"Oh, all right." Irritated, he pulled into the parking lot and turned off the car. "Let's go. Make it quick, though."

We walked in, and I looked around. It had been a long time since I had bought a pair of cowboy boots, but I wandered over to the women's section and had planned to wait until something caught my eye. Immediately, my eyes were drawn to a pair of high-heeled cowboy boots. They were mostly black with a brown upper. Their heels, though not my usual three inches, were respectable. And they were tall—they would fit most of the way to my knee. They were perfect. And very stylish—in a cowboy kind of way.

I found my size, sat down, and tried them on. And of course they fit like the proverbial glove. It's a wrap! They were perfect.

I didn't know where Billy was while I looked and tried on my boots, so I made my way over to the men's section. Billy was nowhere to be seen. Looking toward the front of the store, I checked to see if he was waiting for me by the register. But he wasn't there, either. Finally, I began walking up and down the aisles until I found him in the most unlikely place. The children's section.

"What are you doing?" I asked.

"I found a new pair of boots for me, so I thought I'd get Aiden a matching pair." Billy grinned. "He really liked the other pair that matched mine, so I thought I'd do it again."

"Aiden will love that, Billy."

"Ah, here they are. Let's go now. We have a gun to buy!" He gathered up his boots, Aiden's boots, and my boots, and carried them to the register. In another minute, we were back in the car. Billy had to open the boxes and admire his and Aiden's boots. As an afterthought, he checked mine out as well. At least he looked at them. He admired them, too—I think—and then we were off.

Back on Broadway, we only drove a couple of miles before Billy pulled off onto a side street, and parked in front of a small building that looked like a converted log cabin. There was a wrought iron door that had a cowboy gunfighter group on it, including one gunned cowboy with a suit. It must have been Doc Holliday. Billy opened the iron door and the regular door and invited me in.

I walked to the counter that had guns of all sizes in a locked, glass enclosure. We heard a man's voice in the back that sounded like he was arguing with someone. Billy scowled that no one was there to help us—because he was in a hurry—but he said nothing. So I looked around the large gun shop. On the walls were shelves full of bullets labeled *Ammo* and clips labeled *Magazines*. What—they have their own *gun jargon* here? Whatever. Then a rack of rifles, including some machine-gun types that looked scary, and a rack of purses. Purses! I started making my way to the purses, passing racks of bulletproof vests, gun cases, holsters, ear protection, and displays labeled *Accessories*, that contained knives, binoculars, and flashlights.

Then I heard Billy say, "Hey, Martin! Come on! You have customers out here!"

Martin stuck his head out, looked at Billy and said, "Be right there, Billy. Didn't hear ya come in. Sorry."

Before I reached the purses, Billy called to me from the counter. "Come on, Lor. Let's get the gun first."

Taking one last glance at the purses—which didn't look half bad—I walked back to Billy. Martin was about to walk behind the counter where Billy waited, but his phone rang again, delaying him.

"Where's your purse, Lor?"

"I left it in the car."

He put his hands on my shoulders. "When you get this gun and have it in the purse, you need to keep it with you at all times. All right? I don't want to worry about you not having it. Promise me that you'll always keep it with you."

Martin came out then saving me from making the promise. You know, considering what happened later.

"Martin, I'd like you to meet my wife, Lorry. Lorry, this is my friend, Martin."

"Hi, Martin." He was broad and solid, with a crew cut, and a military demeanor. But he was friendly, and I liked him.

"Hello, Lorry," he said, smiling. Then he turned to Billy. "What can I do for you today, sir?"

I drew my head back and raised my eyebrows at Billy. "Ahem," I said.

Billy and Martin both laughed. "Don't let him fool you, Lor. Martin and I go way back. When we're alone, he calls me *other* names."

"Shhhh!" said Martin. "Don't tell her our secrets!"

Billy looked at his watch. "Anyway, back to business—I need to get back. I came to get Lorry a gun."

"Ah," said Martin. "A lady's gun. One without much recoil."

"Exactly," said Billy.

"These right here are good ones," Martin said while motioning with his hands to the guns in the cabinet by where we were standing.

Looking in, I saw pink guns, blue paisley guns, a gun with some kind of animal print on it, plain gun-looking guns, and then the one I had set my heart on. Yes, already. It had a rosewood handle. It was beautiful and classy, and I wanted it.

CHAPTER THIRTY-SEVEN

"I WANT THAT one, Billy." I pointed to the beauty I was looking at. "The one with the rosewood handle. It's mine."

Billy and Martin both laughed. "Don't you want to hear about the qualities of each?" Billy asked.

"That's what I like. A woman who knows her own mind," said Martin.

"I don't even want a gun!" I said. "But if I have to have one, it's that one."

Martin looked at Billy. "She doesn't want one? Who doesn't want a gun?" The two men shared another laugh.

"I got shot at today, Martin. She *needs* one whether she wants it or not."

"They must have missed, though, right?" Martin inspected Billy head to foot, but he missed the boot.

Billy held up the injured item. "They nicked me right here."

"Oh, that's a close one. I'm glad you're okay, Billy. You wouldn't think that sort of thing happens in Rutledge, though it happens here all the time. Not to change the subject, but did you hear about the fire?"

"What fire?"

"Oh—the fire isn't the real story. A guy's house had a bad fire, and insurance wouldn't let him go in there to get his guns. So what happens? It gets robbed. The guy had a ton of guns—one of my best customers—and they all got stolen. Now they've been showing up in crimes all over Coyote Moon."

Billy shook his head. "I don't suppose you have ballistics on any of them, do you?"

"Naw."

"Too bad," said Billy, holding up a bullet.

That made me look up from admiring my new gun. "You got it!" I said.

"That's not the one from your boot is it?" Martin asked.

"The one from the door of the car." He slipped it back into his pocket. "Tell me about this gun." Billy pointed to *my* new gun.

Martin unlocked the cabinet, pulled it out, and handed it to Billy. "Lady Smith model 60. It's a J frame. Comes with or without a hammer. 5 shot revolver. Uses .38 Specials or .357 Magnum. Less recoil with the .38 Specials."

It seemed time for me to speak up. Less recoil? What if I wanted more of it? Maybe this wasn't the gun for me. "What's recoil?" I asked.

"The backward movement of the gun after it's discharged. It goes up into your arms and pushes on your shoulders."

"Less recoil is a good thing, Lorry. It's definitely what you want."

That is, if I wanted a gun at all. Which I didn't. But I kept quiet. This time. "Ok, that's the one I want." This gun conversation could go on forever if I didn't step in. It was worse than sports talk.

Knowing I didn't have a clue what he was talking about, Martin addressed the next question to Billy. "Do you want one with a hammer or without? I should have both in stock." He turned toward the computer that was to his right on the counter.

"I want one exactly like that." I didn't know what a hammer was, or a nail—if it had to do with guns—but I knew I liked it the way it was.

"Are you sure, Lorry? The one without the hammer won't be as likely to get caught on something in your purse."

"No worries about that, Billy," said Martin. "The concealed carry purses have a zippered compartment that keeps the gun separate."

"Yeah, we need to get the purse!" I started walking over to the purses. Billy followed.

When we got there, Billy said, "Lorry, give Martin your driver's license so he can run it. You don't have any felonies that you never told me about, do you?"

"He's kidding," I said, not taking my eyes off the beautiful, stylish purses. "At least I think he's kidding. Aren't you, Billy? Anyway, it's out in the car with my purse."

"Oh, Lorry! That's right, you told me that. I'll go get it. Martin, give her the official tour of the purses, will you?"

Before Martin got to me, I noticed the different purses: suede, red leather, and a beautiful one with conchos and a western look. That one was perfect.

"I see you already have one picked out, but let me show you these others." He walked around to the other side of the rack. "I don't know if you'd be interested in anything like this, but—" He held out a bright purse that looked like the American flag.

"Ah," I said, "not really my style." Not that I have anything against the American flag, I don't. In fact I love it. Just not on a purse.

"Camo?" he asked.

"Ah, no."

"Is this one bright enough for you?" He held up a hideous orange and green paisley purse that might have been perfect for a day at the beach.

Most of the purses were stylish, but on this side of the aisle, they were in poor taste. Then again, I have high standards. I can't help it. It's genetic. I shook my head no to the paisley purse.

Martin held up a beautiful brown leather trimmed in fake animal fur. "How 'bout this one, Lorry? It comes with a matching gun!"

My eyes got wide. I reached for it as Billy came through the door. "I'll take this one *and* the gun to match!"

"Oh," said Billy. "You changed your mind on the Lady Smith?"

"No. I want them both." I held up both the western purse and the fake animal fur purse.

"You mean both purses, then?" asked Billy, handing Martin my driver's license.

"Well, yes. But I mean both purses *and* both guns."

Billy laughed. "You're quite the salesman, aren't you, Martin? She didn't even want one gun when we came in here, and now you're sending her home with two!"

As Martin typed away at the keys on the computer, he said, "Billy, the second gun is a Walther CCP 9mm. That okay with you?"

"That should have more recoil, but she can handle it. Yeah, wrap 'em both up, and some ammo, too. And Martin, while you're typing, can you tell Lorry when you started your son on guns and why?"

"Sure." Martin nodded toward me and continued. "I started him on airsoft guns when he was three. When he handled those properly, I moved him on. At six, he could break down and disarm a weapon." He shrugged and continued. "My philosophy is give them guns to kill their curiosity about them. Knowing how to handle a gun is as important as learning how to swim. They can both kill ya." Martin finished typing and looked up. "I probably don't need to ask you this, Billy, but does she have her permit yet?"

"Driver's?" I asked, innocently, though I knew he didn't mean that.

"No, concealed carry," he said to me. And then to Martin, "Not yet. I'll either give her the class myself after I finish this case, or I'll bring her to your next one. I'll let you know." Then he turned back to me, "Lorry, you keep this purse and gun with you!"

"Yes, sir," I said as I saluted with the hand that wasn't admiring the feel of my beautiful new purses.

CHAPTER THIRTY-EIGHT

BILLY KISSED ME goodbye and drove off back to work. He said he didn't think he'd be home for dinner, so I was on my own. And I knew exactly where I would go.

Bingo and I entered the back door of the historical society and walked up to the front. Petra was typing away on her keyboard.

"Everything all right, Petra? Want to see my new purses?"

"I thought you went to buy a gun?" she asked without turning around. And it sounded like she didn't slow down her typing, either.

"I did, but I needed a purse to carry it in. It's called a concealed carry purse. Want to see it? Well, two of them."

"No, that's okay. I'm good. Purses aren't my thing, you know."

"How about the guns? Want to see the guns? They're pretty, too."

"A pretty gun? No, I don't think so. I've never considered a gun pretty, and I don't think I've been missing out on anything. Thanks for offering, though."

"Hey, Petra. You want to go out to dinner tonight? Billy has to work."

"Thanks, Lorry, but I'm going back to the bed and breakfast. There are some guests from England, so I should be there. Thanks for asking."

"I can bring pizza," I tempted.

"No, Hugo left some stuff for me."

"All right," I said and walked into my office. I tried. Petra did seem a little better today. Almost back to her old self. If she had insulted me, that would be just about there.

It was almost time to leave for the day—not that I had been there much, but with the sale still threatening, what difference did it make? After turning off my computer and gathering up my new purses and my dog, I was ready to take off when Petra raced by me.

"Want a ride home to pick up some stuff? Then I can drop you at Martha's."

"No, thanks. I have everything I need, and the walk will do me good."

It was only a few blocks walk to Martha's, but I would have accepted a ride. Maybe that was why Petra was so thin you could almost see through her, and I was, well, I just wasn't—you know, thin. "Okay, bye! See you tomorrow!"

"Bye. See ya," then she was out the door and striding down the street with her long legs.

"Bingo, what d'ya say we blow this pop stand?" Bingo put his two front feet up on my lap. "Let's get outa here!" I gathered him up in my arms, locked the front door, and rambled down the hallway toward my car.

The back door to the historical society locked by itself. Billy had that fixed after we had a problem or two with the back door. Bingo and I jumped into my car, and we were off. "Bingo," I said, "we're not going home yet. You have to wait on your dinner. I hope you can adjust." He wagged, so I took that as assent.

Which bar would rich Douglas Gates be at? The nicer one? No, that would be too logical, and nothing about this case was logical. So I drove to Petey's Bar, a cesspool of a place where no respectable drunk would be caught dead. Drunk? Yes. Dead? No. Wait a minute. Grizelda's, another nicer bar in town also served food that wasn't half bad. We ate there sometimes. My gut feeling was that Douglas Gates wouldn't be there. Petey's was a total dump. Petra's alcoholic father hung out there, and I hoped that I wouldn't run into him on this *mission.*

The bar, located at the end of Commercial Street and way too close to the school—Aiden's school—to suit me, needed painting. I snagged a parking place right in front—convenient in case I needed to make a quick getaway. After kissing Bingo on the top of his head, I grabbed my new concealed carry purse, even though I didn't even know how to load the gun yet. Billy said he'd show me when he got home tonight.

Petey's was a dive, and if I got into trouble, even waving the gun around might save me some grief—or worse. It wouldn't reflect very good on Billy to have his newly wedded wife waving a gun around in the worst bar in Rutledge. But right now, the only thing on my mind was finding the murderer.

And that might be Douglas Gates. So I opened the door to Petey's Bar and looked around the room. It didn't take long to find him. He sat at the counter on the end seat and leaned against the wall. If he was already drunk, then I wouldn't be able to get much out of him. On the other hand, if he was drunk enough, he might *confide* in me about his part in the murder. Think positive! He would spill!

I glided across the floor toward Douglas—as if hanging out in bars was something I did all the time—and plunked myself down in the empty seat next to him. "Hello, Douglas," I said, trying to sound innocent and unassuming. Then, trying to play my part correctly, I held up a finger to the bartender.

Since I wasn't a barfly and hadn't ever spent much time in a bar before, I didn't know how to act. But I thought holding up a finger was the way to do it. Since I didn't know what to order, I ordered the only thing I could think of, which came from some movie I once saw. I couldn't remember which one. "Martini, please. Shaken not stirred." The bartender looked at me with a weird expression on his face and grabbed a bottle. What he did with it, I didn't know, because it was then that Douglas spoke.

"So what are you doing in this God forsaken place, Lorry? That's your name, isn't it? Lorry Lockharte? You're the one who made a spectacle of yourself at that meeting. That was you, wasn't it?"

"Yes, and that, kind sir, is why I need a drink!" The bartender put the drink down in front of me, and I handed him a ten. He tried to give me change, but I indicated he should keep it. He tipped a pretend hat to me and smiled. Bob is what his name tag said, and he had pimples all over his face. It was probably syphilis or something. I hoped he washed his hands before washing the glasses. I pretended to take a sip of my drink and then wiped the liquid off my lip so I wouldn't ingest any.

Douglas moved from the wall and leaned up against me, drowning me with his alcoholic breath. "So who do you think did it? You know, the murder, I mean." He took a gulp of his drink.

"You!" I said, looking him as much in the eye as I could with him leaning against me. I might as well speak my mind, because he was too drunk to remember anything I said, anyway.

He laughed and alcohol burbled out of his mouth. With no napkin before him, he wiped it on the sleeve of his very expensive looking suit. "I couldn't have done it! I don't have a gun!" And he took another gulp, then laughed again, so the liquid came out his nose. He wiped this new impropriety on his other sleeve.

Douglas had said it so matter-of-factly, that it took me aback. That would be a prerequisite, wouldn't it? Although, after what Martin had said about those guns being stolen, Douglas could have easily done it and gotten rid of the evidence afterward. "All right then," I said. "Where were you at the time?"

"Just outside the front door, behind a bush so I couldn't be seen."

I turned toward him and his head slid off my shoulder where it had been resting. He almost fell over, but caught himself in time. With his comment, my mind had gone to the toilet, literally. "Why did you have to take a leak outside behind a bush? Was the men's bathroom busy?"

"No, silly! For this!" And he reached into his inside pocket and pulled out a stainless steel flask of alcohol. After holding it up for me to see, he returned it to his pocket, finished his drink, and ordered another one. "And another for the lady, too." He motioned toward me.

Douglas hadn't noticed that I hadn't drank any of the martini in front of me, which was a good thing, but the bartender did. He looked at me, and I discreetly shook my head. When he brought Douglas his drink and no other, Douglas did notice that. "I said, bring her another drink! Can't you hear, boy?"

Bob shrugged, and made and handed me another martini. I assumed it was also shaken and not stirred, but I didn't ask.

As far out as it seemed, I believed Douglas. He could be faking the whole thing, except that he didn't know I'd be visiting him tonight, and he was already leaning against the wall before I even sat down beside him. And that alcoholic breath of his wasn't from just one or two drinks. No, I thought he was the first one that I could officially take off my list. Excited at the thought, I was about to stand up and take my leave, but Douglas leaned back over.

"You know what, missy? Everybody in town thinks that I'm related to Bill Gates. I don't know where they'd ever get that idea." He raised his eyebrows and glanced briefly away before leaning in again. "Just a rumor." In that moment and in that one comment, I knew without his saying another word that *he* had started that rumor. Some things are obvious.

Then he continued, "You know where I made all my money?" He turned his mouth so he could whisper in my ear with his drunken breath. "High end mobile home parks. I have two of them in Oregon. You know, taxes. I've made a fortune off those." He pulled away from me and looked concerned. "You won't tell anyone, will you? I mean, I prefer the rumor!"

That was when I stood up. "No, Douglas. I won't tell a soul." Except maybe the Rutledge weekly newspaper. "Goodbye!" And I shimmied my big butt straight out the door and into the waiting paws of my boy, Bingo.

CHAPTER THIRTY-NINE

COLOR ME SLIMED. At least that's how I felt. Being in that crummy bar, and Bob the bartender handing me a drink washed with possibly dirty hands, and finally Douglas's alcoholic breath all over me. If there was a cleaners still open in Rutledge—there wasn't—but if there was, I would drive over there right now, rip my clothes off, and drive home naked. Okay, okay, I wouldn't do that, but you get how gross I felt at that moment.

When I arrived home, I put Bingo in the backyard to do his business, tore my clothes off, and stuffed them in a plastic bag for transportation to the cleaners in the morning. Then I showered and scrubbed myself hard enough to make my skin red. After toweling off and letting Bingo in, I put on a warm robe and put some leftover frozen pizza in the microwave. A few minutes later, I was enjoying pizza and feeling relatively clean. The only thing that still felt dirty about me were thoughts about that horrible place. So I let it go and called Aiden.

After going through both Willow, Sam's daughter, and Sage, Sam's son, I finally had Aiden on the phone. "Hi, sweetie, are you having a good time? . . . Good, I'm glad you enjoy each other's company . . . Yes, I know he's smart, and you are, too . . . You talk about science? That is very cool. . . . Stay for the whole weekend? Are you sure it's okay with Sage's folks? . . . Oh, sorry, you're right. I should have known you wouldn't have asked unless you already had permission. . . . I love you, too, Aiden."

And of course you can stay there. . . . All right, give me a call sometime. Love you."

During the whole conversation, I resisted the urge to ask him if the gun was unloaded. I deserve a pat on the back! Either that or a slap in the face for not trusting Billy and his conversation with Sage's parents. And not to mention the lock on the gun.

Walking toward my bedroom, I noticed Billy had dropped off more empty boxes. He had my whole evening planned. Since I didn't know how soon we were moving into the new house, I didn't know if I should pack our dresser or not. Who knew how long it would take for Billy to catch the murderer and for Martha and Hugo to return home? Little did I know how soon it would be.

Instead of working in the bedroom, I started packing the books and drawers in the office. By the time Billy arrived home hours later, I had filled all the boxes and fallen asleep with my butt on the floor and my head on the office chair. When I awoke, Billy had knelt down beside me, and I could feel the warmth of his hands on my face.

"Hey, Babe, you did a lot of work tonight. You must be tired." He tactfully ignored how he found me sleeping on the floor. I nodded.

"We need to get these boxes to the new house. If you see Mason around tomorrow, ask him if he could help. My truck will be here, just have him load them in there."

"Ok." I struggled to get the sleep from my tired brain. "When are we moving in? Don't you have to catch the guy, first?"

"I'm getting closer. It shouldn't be long now." He stood up and offered me his hand. "Come on, let's get you to bed before you fall back to sleep on the floor."

"No! You said you'd show me how to load the guns!"

Billy pulled me to my feet and put his arms around me. "For someone who didn't even want a gun, you're getting into this gun thing. First, you buy two instead of one, and now you're eager to learn how to load them, even though you're about to fall asleep on your feet!"

"I'm not that tired!" I argued, though I could feel Billy half holding me up.

"How 'bout a compromise?" he asked. "I'll show you how to load *one* of the guns tonight. How 'bout that?"

I nodded and rested my head on Billy's shoulder. "Ok."

Billy put his arm around me and kept me upright while we walked into the living room. He eased me down onto the couch, and I sank right in. "I'll get the gun and the ammo. Wait here, and try not to fall asleep," he said as he headed back down the hall toward the bedroom where I had left the guns.

When he returned a minute later, I felt more wide awake. "Did you bring both guns? Because I'm feeling a lot more awake now."

"You agreed to one. I brought the Lady Smith. Your fancy Cheetah CCP has a magazine. It's easy to load." Billy sat down beside me with the gun in his hand. I didn't see the bullets. "Before we begin, just a brief gun safety lesson. Are you awake enough to retain the information?"

I frowned and sighed. "I'm awake enough for a ten-question quiz. Now get on with it, Billy." Maybe I did feel more tired than I thought, because I usually didn't talk to Billy like that.

Billy narrowed his eyes but said nothing about my curt response. He knew how tired I was, too. "First, always treat *every* gun like it's loaded. Don't ever pick it up and wave it around "pretending" to shoot someone. More people have been shot by *unloaded guns*—guns they *thought* were unloaded—than you would believe."

Billy held the gun up and ran his finger along the business end of it. "This is called the muzzle of the gun. Always point the muzzle in a safe direction. If the gun accidentally goes off, you don't want to destroy anything or hurt anybody."

He had it pointed toward our empty kitchen. I hoped it wouldn't go off and kill the refrigerator. I liked that refrigerator.

"All right. Still listening?" When I nodded my head, he continued. "Never put your finger on the trigger until you are ready to shoot the gun. See where my finger is?" I was going to make a

smart-aleck comment but wisely kept my mouth shut and nodded again. He had stretched his index finger straight out against
the gun above where the trigger was. "Now here is your ten-
question quiz in one question. Repeat what I told you."

Raising my eyebrows in an exasperated expression, I repeated
what he said almost verbatim. That impressed him. Smiling, he
pulled the bullets from his shirt pocket and dropped them into
his lap. Then he held up the other side of the gun, with it pointed
toward the other side of the house. The refrigerator was now
safe.

"The first thing you do is make sure the hammer is not in a
cocked position. This is the hammer and this is cocked." With his
thumb, he pulled the hammer back until it clicked, then he
pulled it again and lowered it back to where it started. "See
this?" He indicated a small button on the side of the gun. "Push
the cylinder release forward with your thumb while you push
the cylinder out with your other fingers."

He held the gun up in front of my face with the muzzle pointed to the ceiling. "See? You can see that it is unloaded. Now, take
the bullets and insert the pointed end of the bullet into the
chamber. Press it gently until it is fully seated. Do the same thing
with all five bullets. Then snap the cylinder back in place like
this. All done! Now let's go to bed!"

Billy started to get up, but I pulled him back down. "I want to
try it. I'm a tactile learner." He sighed but handed me the pretty
rosewood handle of my new gun. Pointing it in a safe direction, I
held it in my hand, pushed the cylinder release with my thumb
and then pushed it out. "Oh! It's loaded. How do I unload it?"

"Here. Press that and turn the gun so the bullets come out."
He pointed to something sticking straight up. "It's called either a
cylinder plunger or an ejector rod."

I pushed it and the bullets fell into my lap. Then I checked the
cylinder to make sure no bullets remained, closed it up, and
began again. After I had loaded it and unloaded it several times,
I handed it back to Billy.

"Can we go to sleep now, please?" he asked.

I nodded, we walked into the bedroom, and both of us fell immediately asleep. It would have been a very restful night except for the gunshot that awoke us around midnight.

CHAPTER FORTY

AT FIRST, I thought it was a dream since I had been loading and unloading my new gun right before I went to sleep. But when I felt Billy jump out of bed, I knew it wasn't. Then I thought I had loaded the gun incorrectly causing it to discharge by itself. When Billy ran right past my concealed carry purse and grabbed his sheriff's station radio, I knew it wasn't that, either.

"Nick! Nick! What's going on? Do you need me?" he whispered into his radio. If he was trying not to wake me, it was way too late for that. The gunshot sounded close. "All right. All right. If you need me, just call."

He put the radio down and climbed back into bed beside me. Seeing that I was awake, he said, "One single gunshot, no reports yet. He said when he gets a report, he'll go out, and if he needs me, he'll call." Billy kissed me. "So, for now, let's go back to sleep." And we did.

Billy was restless for the rest of the night. I could feel him shifting in bed, this way and that. When first light of morning came, he was already dressed and ready to go. He leaned over to kiss me goodbye. "I'll call you when I find out anything," and he was out the door.

I thought I'd have a leisurely morning at home, since I didn't have to make Aiden's lunch or make sure he was ready for school. As I stepped out of the shower, Billy called. "Come to the sheriff's station? Now? . . . Why? . . . Why can't you tell me

164

now? . . . All right, all right. I'll get dressed right now and drive over. I don't get why you need me for sheriff's work, though. . . . Or maybe it's because I'm such an old hand with a gun and you need me as back up!" Billy didn't laugh at my joke. We said goodbye and hung up.

Billy's voice, besides the lack of humor, sounded serious and concerned. And there was an edge to it I hadn't heard before. Hurrying, I got dressed, collected Bingo, and we were off. The sheriff's station was only minutes away, and when I got there, Billy was outside waiting for me.

He walked over to my car window, and I pressed the button to roll it down. "Listen, I don't have time to explain. Follow me, and you'll know what to do." Then he walked away and got into his sheriff's car.

The whole thing was getting weirder and weirder, or curiouser and curiouser as I sometimes like to say. A few minutes later, Billy pulled into a driveway I knew well. It was Martha and Hugo's bed and breakfast. Oh, no. Please don't let anything have happened to Martha or Hugo, I thought. It took a second to remember they were both safe and staying at our new ranch.

Billy jumped out of his sheriff's car and then opened the door to my car. He reached in to help me out. "C'mon," he said, and repeated, "You'll know what to do." Grabbing my hand, we marched together up to the door where he rang the bell.

A man with an English accent answered the door, and Billy asked if Petra was around. The man said she was upstairs getting ready for work, but he'd tell her someone was there to see her. Before he hopped up the stairs two by two, he turned and said, "She might be running a little late this morning. I'm afraid my wife and I had her up half the night playing cards." I wondered what he was thinking—having a sheriff come to the door asking for his host at the bed and breakfast. I didn't even know what to think.

Billy leaned over and whispered in my ear, "Petra's father killed himself last night. That was the gunshot we heard."

But I didn't have time to process the information before Petra came bounding down the stairs with a big smile on her face. "What?" she asked. "I'm late for work one time and you have to bring your sheriff boyfriend—excuse me, I mean husband—out to fetch me?"

By that time, she stood right in front of us, and Billy put his hands on her shoulders. "Petra, you were up late last night. Did you hear the gunshot?"

"Yeah. We were playing cards. We all heard it. So what?"

"I'm sorry, Petra. Your father shot himself. He's gone."

She took a step backward and looked at him. And although I expected to see a look of grief on her face, what I saw instead looked more like relief. The guy was a lowlife drunk who sometimes beat her mother, but still, you'd think she would feel some grief. He was her father.

"I'm so sorry, Petra," is all I could think of to say.

"My mom. What's she going to do now?" Petra said in disbelief. "As much of a jerk as he was, I don't know what she'll do without him. She depended on him."

Billy reached out and drew her to him. "She'll be fine, Petra. She'll get along fine. Probably better off than she was with him. You, too." And as much as that didn't sound like something you would say to someone who just lost their father, it seemed to make Petra feel better. Billy always knew the right thing to say.

"Yes," she said. "You're right. Mom will be better off without him, and so will I."

CHAPTER FORTY-ONE

"YOU DON'T HAVE to come into work today, Petra," I said and reached out to hug her. It was brief, though, because she pulled away before I had finished. I hate when that happens.

"Oh, no. I'll be in for sure," she said without a trace of grief. Although maybe that was my imagination. "I have to call my mom and finish getting ready. Then I'll be in." She turned to Billy. "Thank you for coming to tell me, Billy. I'm glad it was you." She flashed a mild smile in my direction. "You, too, Lorry. See ya soon." She turned around and fairly skipped up the stairs.

At that moment, I thought to myself it was a good thing she had a solid alibi, because her behavior was not only curious, it made her seem downright guilty. I wondered if her father really had committed suicide.

Billy put his arm around me and led me outside, where he walked me to my car. "Thank you for coming with me, Lor."

"I don't think you needed me, Billy. Petra took it well, don't you think? Almost too well?" The last word rose up in a pointed question.

"Now, Lorry, there you go again jumping to conclusions. Different people show grief in different ways. Don't judge her because she doesn't conform to your standards."

He was right, so I nodded and slipped behind the wheel of my car. My new concealed carry purse sat on the floor of the passenger side. Billy hadn't even noticed I didn't have it with me, even after I had told him I would always carry it.

"I doubt if this has anything to do with whoever shot at me, but stranger things have happened. I'm running the bullet through ballistics, just in case." Billy leaned over to kiss me. "I'll see ya later, sweetie." He closed the door of my car and strode back to his.

Bingo and I drove to the historical society and parked. I thought that checking the ballistics was a waste of time. I had heard suicide sometimes ran in families, and I knew Petra's brother had committed suicide. We entered the building and walked toward my front office. It felt strange not seeing Petra there, because she usually arrived before me. She wasn't late, though, because it was still early. And I was hungry. Very hungry. I had left in such a hurry at Billy's request that I hadn't had coffee or anything to eat.

After turning on my computer, I grabbed my newly acquired concealed carry purse, very stylish I might add, and slid out the front door, locking it behind me. Bingo sat in my chair, feet on my desk, watching me walk by. I smiled at him.

When I walked inside the Koffee Korner Kafe, the first thing I noticed were the two people sitting at the counter: Paul Gallagher and Elizabeth Conroy. They were probably planning another murder! Who would it be this time? The son! He was the next one that had to go so they could continue with their evil plans—whatever they were. I'd have to warn Billy.

I hiked right up to them and said, "So I see you two are here together planning the next murder!" Honestly, I think my mouth sometimes—ok! often!—engages before my brain. I hadn't planned to say that. Really.

Kasey, standing at the cash register said, "No, Elizabeth just sat down, and she asked Paul if she should get the caramel mocha latte or the pumpkin spice."

"Oh. Well. How about a coffee and one of those egg sandwich things?" I used to ask for an Egg McMuffin thing, but Kasey always refused to acknowledge what I meant.

"Hello, Lorry," said Elizabeth with a slight smile on her face.

"Lorry," said Paul without looking at me.

"So we are both still on your list of suspects?" Elizabeth asked with a sly grin.

"Nobody is off my list," I said defensively. "Besides, you already told me it could be you."

"Yes, I did. Doesn't the fact that Paul and I were both at the bulletin board—so we could alibi each other—plus the fact that we saw Douglas walk by, well, wouldn't that clear the three of us? Lorry, it would help to solve the crime if you could narrow your suspect list down, don't you think?"

She was always so objective and insightful, but I wouldn't give her the satisfaction of telling her that. In her presence, I again felt like a high school student in front of the principal. So I answered her in the only logical way I could. "Whatever!" I said as I stuck my nose in the air, paid for my sandwich and coffee, and exited the Kafe.

Sitting down at my desk, I took the top off the coffee and put the cup to my lips. Mmmm mmmm good. Despite the questionable company, that place had good coffee and good food. I took a bite of sandwich and said it again, mmmm mmmm. Then I noticed Bingo was nowhere around. "Bingo? Come here Bingo!"

"He's in here with me, Lorry," said Petra.

Petra's here! That surprised me. Although I knew she said she was coming in, I didn't expect her. Putting the sandwich down, I wiped my fingers on a napkin, took another sip of coffee, and walked to the other room.

Bingo was in her arms licking her face, and she didn't look half bad for someone who had just lost their father to suicide. I put my arms out to hug her, but she held up her hand.

"No need. I'm doing fine. Honestly. Fine. Mid-thirteenth century. Meaning unblemished, free of impurities. That's me. Unblemished." Then she blushed, put her head into Bingo's fur, and I thought I saw a stray tear fall.

"Are you sure you want to be here, Petra? You don't need to be, you know."

Petra kissed Bingo, set him down on the floor, and turned to her computer that already displayed the spreadsheet she was working on. "I'm fine."

And that was that. Bingo and I returned to my office; and I finished my breakfast, enjoying every sip of coffee and every bite of sandwich. It was so good, I considered going back for more. I patted my generous tummy. No, probably not a good idea.

I sat facing the fish tank enjoying my sandwich and the smooth movements of the fish when I heard a sound outside I thought I recognized. Turning in my chair, I looked out the window and saw Mason. He put his motorcycle on the kickstand and bounded to the door and inside. "Hi, Lorry," he said in passing, without even looking at me.

I heard Petra's chair move and imagined her standing up to greet him. "Are you all right?" he asked.

She must have nodded, because the next thing I heard was, "How'd you know?"

"Billy called me," Mason replied.

And they started whispering, because I couldn't hear another word, even with my hand to my ear which extended the hearing radius much farther than normal. There's a reason guard dogs have such tall ears. And yes, I admit I tried to listen. Is that so wrong of me? So sue me.

I took my time finishing my breakfast and then turned back to my desk and computer. Mason and Petra were still whispering in the other room. That wasn't unusual—they often did that when Mason came to visit. After checking my email, I stood up and walked back there.

They were still standing up and hugging. I said, "You're welcome to leave, Petra. You two can go back to the bed and breakfast or go home."

I would have added more, but Petra pulled away from Mason and looked at me with fire shooting from her eyes. It looked like she was ticked off at me, but I had no idea why. She *was* a teenager, though, and teenagers were unpredictable; and on this day she was a teenager who had just been through a traumatic event.

"I'm *never* going back to that house! I don't care if I have to live on the street!" Then she turned back to Mason and fell back into his arms.

So I walked away. What could I say after that? Even I, moi, sometimes run out of smart-aleck comments. And it didn't seem appropriate, anyway. Not that I've let that stop me before. But still.

CHAPTER FORTY-TWO

DECIDING TO GO back to my list of suspects, I opened the middle drawer on the left-hand side of the desk and pulled out the paper I had been working on before. All the suspects were in alphabetical order by first names, and I hadn't crossed out a single one. That was about to change.

When I was a kid and used to play the game called Clue, I always lost. You know why? I refused to guess. If I wasn't *positive* that Colonel Mustard did it with the candlestick in the library, then I would wait until I was sure. Trouble was that other kids who didn't have half the information I had—but were willing to guess—guessed right and won the game. I always used to think—what if I was wrong? And I didn't like to be wrong. Now the stakes were even higher. Kind of. Although I'd solved a few cases, Billy had always been right there solving it the same time I did.

Anyway, let's start crossing out names based on the meager amount of information I have. Anthony Petrelli? No, I refuse to cross him out. Then I happened to glance out the window and there on the other side of the street—having come out of the hardware store—walked short, squat Anthony Petrelli with a tall, blonde bombshell. I watched as he put his hand around her waist and then sneaked that same hand down and pinched her on the butt.

"Ha!" I declared. "I knew he was a womanizer!"

A few minutes before, I had heard Mason's big feet trudging down the hallway toward the bathroom, and now I heard Petra's light step come up behind me. She leaned over my shoulder and peered out the window. "Anthony Petrelli? Womanizer? No, Lorry. Sorry to ruin your assumptions, but that woman is his wife, and he is *devoted* to her. They came to talk about relationships in my Psychology class last year. You should see the way they look at each other. Those two are *in love*. He's not the screwaround type. Sorry to disappoint you." She patted me on the shoulder and returned to her desk.

Grumbling, I crossed Anthony's name off the list. Officially. Although I didn't know where he was during the murder—and that was my own fault—the only thing I had on him was he thought Martha did it. Sad to say, they *all* thought that, though for what reason I'll never know.

If I knew who had voted for the sale and who didn't, it would help me analyze the information I had. A chill ran down my spine. It was so distinct that I thought Mason had poured cold water down my back, but when I turned around, I heard him in the other room talking to Petra. Still, I felt the back of my dress— my dark blue dress with light blue trim—to be sure. It was dry. The reason I felt the chill was that I wondered if I had been off track the whole time with this case. Suppose someone killed Christopher Fenton for a reason *other* than the sale of the historical society. Now *that* was a provocative notion.

Okay, moving on. Brent Lindsay. He didn't go to the meeting condemning Martha, which I thought was a good thing. If the motive for the murder had nothing to do with the sale, then would that even mean anything? Were the two related at all— not condemning Martha and the sale? I didn't know. So I wouldn't cross him out yet.

Next, Christa Hawthorne. My whole reasoning for keeping her on the list was so stupid that I was ashamed of myself. I put the pen next to her name ready to cross her off, when—surprise of surprises—she walked past my window, put her hand on the door, and strolled right in. I slid the suspect list under another piece of paper on my desk and turned to face her.

Christa, dressed in an expensive light and dark brown pantsuit, wore heels that were taller than mine. That's reason enough to keep her on the list! Oh, wait. She stood above me and said, "I heard that shot last night. Was it related to the ones the other day?"

Since it was just Christa, it didn't bother me having her stand above me like that. If it had been Elizabeth Conroy, I would have stood up in an instant. My concealed carry purse was on the floor beside me, because I had neglected to put it in the drawer when I returned from the Kafe next door. It didn't escape my notice, though, how Christa gave it a second look. "Shhh," I whispered and pointed to the other room, where thankfully I heard Mason and Petra still talking. She leaned down and I whispered in her ear, "It was Petra's father who committed suicide last night."

"Oh, well, that's too bad, but it's good that it wasn't related to the other shooting." She said it in an even tone with no compassion. That was weird. Maybe she had a bad relationship with her father, too, like Petra.

"Probably not, but Billy's doing ballistics on it, anyway. See if it matches the other bullets."

Christa took a step backward with an awkward expression on her face. Maybe she twisted her ankle on those too-tall heels. A person can only hope. Wait, that wasn't nice. She said, "Oh, I didn't think they ever found those bullets."

I shrugged. "Musta found one. I don't know." Something felt weird about the conversation, though I couldn't figure out what it was.

"Well, I best be going now." She opened the door, then turned back. "Nice talking to you, Lorry," she said with a genuine smile on her face. If nothing else, Christa was pleasant. That had to count for something.

She walked by my window on the way back to her shop, and I turned my chair so I could check my email. The wheeled chair moved a little to the side and Bingo cried out when the wheel hit his toe. "Bingo! I'm sorry! What are you doing there, anyway?" Usually, he lay at my feet on the other side of the desk. That was curious. Bingo jumped into my lap and licked his paw. I checked, but it wasn't cut or anything. So I kissed it to make him feel better. He might have been on the other side of my chair because he was afraid that Christa would step on him with those spiky heels!

After petting him for enough time to forget his injury and wag his tail, I was about to reach for the suspect list when I saw Billy's patrol car pull up out front. Bingo jumped off my lap, and I stood up in anticipation of a hug. Billy rushed in and gave me half a hug as he walked toward Petra's office. "Where's Mason? I saw his bike out front."

"In the bathroom," was Petra's reply.

And I thought, again? He had spent more time in the bathroom than he had with Petra this morning.

Billy turned around and came back to me, but didn't finish the hug. "Ask him if he can come to the house tomorrow and help you load the boxes, take 'em to the new house, and unload them there. I'll pay him, of course."

"As if he'd let you!" said Petra from the other room.

Hearing her voice again, Billy walked back in there. "Are you all right, Petra?"

"She's got her snark back if that's any indication," I said, still stinging a little from the half a hug.

"I'm doing good, Billy. Honest, I'm okay. Mason will stay with me for the afternoon and will stay at the bed and breakfast tonight. I'll be fine."

I wanted to tell her not to bother explaining the etymology of the word fine, but I kept my mouth closed for once. And it was a good idea. Billy walked back and before going out the door, he gave me a big hug and a kiss on the lips. "I love you, and in case you didn't figure it out, I'll be working tomorrow." Then he opened the door and was about to step through. He held up his thumb and forefinger a half inch apart. "I'm this close, Lor, *this* close. See ya late tonight. Don't wait up. Love you, bye." And he disappeared out the door.

CHAPTER FORTY-THREE

"I'LL TELL MASON for you, Lorry. I'm sure he'll do it—if I encourage him. He's fussing over me right now, which I don't mind."

"It's okay with you if he's away for a few hours tomorrow? There are a lot of boxes to move."

"I'm fine. You know, fine."

"Not again, Petra. But thanks."

After putting my concealed carry purse into the drawer where it belonged, I clicked on my email. Nothing there, so I did something that I only rarely did. I surfed the Net. Since I had just put my purse away, I thought I might as well see what else was out there. So I clicked on some links for concealed carry purses and saw some beautiful ones that weren't expensive—not that I needed to look at prices anymore, but once you've lived in poverty, you get into the habit. And being frugal never hurt anybody either.

Hours later, after one click led to another and led to a hundred more, I was still immersed in what cool concealed carry purses were out there when I heard the door open. In walked Zack James. "Hi, Lorry," he said with a slight smile on his face.

Zack, dressed in new blue jeans, a dress shirt, and a suit jacket, looked better every time I saw him. And I felt very grateful that I had stood up for him when I hardly even knew him. With Zack, it made a huge difference. That's satisfaction.

"Hi, Zack." I smiled back.

"Is Petra here? I heard about what happened, so I didn't think she would be, but I saw Mason's bike out front."

"I'm in here, Zack!" Petra called from her office.

Zack shrugged his shoulders, touched my arm affectionately, and walked to the back. "Hi, Petra. How are you holding up?"

"I'm doing fine, Zack."

"Where's Mason? I saw his bike out front."

"He has some stomach thing going on. He's in the bathroom. We're going out to dinner tonight. You want to go with us?"

I heard Zack demurring to the suggestion, and then heard Mason's voice boom out, "Zack, my man! You goin' with us tonight to celebrate?"

Barely above a whisper, I heard Petra say, "Mason, that's inappropriate."

Then Zack said, "Well, I'm glad you're okay, Petra. I'll see you both later sometime. Bye."

As Zack walked past me and said goodbye, he shrugged his shoulders, like, "I have no idea."

I was going to return to surfing the 'net, but I turned toward the fish so I could think about this. It was such a peculiar thing to say. *Celebrate?* Her father was *dead*. Yes, he was a jerk and a scoundrel, but in death, didn't he deserve some respect for his paternal role in her birth?

I didn't know what the answer to that should be. Never having been beaten or having to watch as my father beat my mother, it was a judgment I couldn't make. Although I know I'm good at judging, in this case, I couldn't do it. The subject was too sensitive, too *hot*, as they say. And I was staying out of it. So I turned back to my desk and pulled out the suspect list.

Putting Petra and her father out of my mind, I began to focus on the list. All right, so I had crossed Anthony Petrelli out, as much as I didn't want to. Brent Lindsay was still on the live list. Christa, I had been about to cross her out before she came to visit, but now, I wasn't so sure. She'd stay live for now. Next was Douglas Gates, and I crossed him out. Sneaking a drink during the murder may be distasteful, but I didn't think he murdered anyone. Elizabeth Conroy, off the list, along with Paul Gallagher. Joe, the mayor, already off the list. He had what they call an ironclad alibi: me!

Russ Tabor. If the murder had nothing to do with the sale of the historical society, which I was becoming more and more convinced of, Russ would make more sense than anyone else— especially since he was on the team blaming Martha for the crime. Get her out of the way, then he could take over as the town manager. The murder of Christopher Fenton would have been to get Martha in trouble. He had worked with her for years, so I could understand that he wouldn't want to *kill* her, but he could get her out of the way by killing someone else and *blaming* her. It made perfect sense. Russ had just jumped to my number one suspect.

Wait a minute, though. Last on the list was Todd Fenton, the dead man's son. Now that I was looking at motive differently, I had to look at Todd Fenton differently. He, even more than Russ Tabor, had something to gain by having his father dead. Money. And greed was always a powerful motive. And where had he said he was? He said he went to the men's room and was supposed to meet his father back in the conference room. Not what I would call a strong alibi. It was barely a weak alibi. It wasn't an alibi at all! Todd just jumped to the top of my suspect list. It was him. I knew it was.

CHAPTER FORTY-FOUR

AFTER MY REMARKABLE deduction that Todd Fenton was the killer, as I silently gloated at how brilliant to have come up with that, Aiden called. He said he missed me and told me all about his weekend plans with his friend Sage. Then he said he had to go, and I told him how much I missed him and loved him. We hung up with me feeling a shred of regret that he was already growing up enough to spend the whole weekend without me. But that's part of life, isn't it?

"Hey, Lorry," Mason said, as he and Petra walked up to my desk on their way out. It was already five o'clock, and I had wasted the entire afternoon. "Petra mentioned that Billy wanted me to help move some boxes tomorrow. Sure. What time do you want me there?"

"Not too early. How about ten, then afterward I can buy you lunch?"

"That sounds fine. Just have a pizza delivered to the bed and breakfast so I can share it with my girl." He gave Petra's shoulder a squeeze, and she eked out a smile.

"All right. Will do. I'll see ya tomorrow at ten." Then I focused on Petra. "I'm sorry again, Petra, about your Dad."

She raised her right hand as if brushing it away, and Mason led her out the door. It made me ponder again what Mason had said about going out to celebrate. That gave me the chills. Standing up, I stepped to the front door, locked it, and turned the sign to closed. I leaned over to retrieve my concealed carry purse from the drawer, gave Bingo a quick pat while I was down there, and was about to take off when the phone rang.

Dang. It was 5:01. Should I get it? Whatever it is, it should be quick, because we were already closed. So I answered, thankfully. It was Billy saying he had time for a quick bite if I could meet him in ten minutes at Grizelda's Bar and Grill. Yes! I read over my list one last time, nodded my head again at my brilliant deduction, and then Bingo and I were out the back door and into the car in a flash.

Grizelda's was on Church Street with Rutledge Market on one side and Petrelli's car lot on the other. I know that it sounded weird that a bar would be on the same street as a church, but in all good conscience, I had to point out that Grizelda's was probably there first—before it was called Church Street. This was a former old west town, you know. A person has to expect these sorts of things in an old west town. Or at least that's what I've been told.

I could barely contain my excitement about *discovering* the murderer! And I couldn't wait to tell Billy! He'd be so happy with me! What am I saying? *I'm* happy with me! We parked in the parking lot, and although Billy had said ten minutes and it wasn't even five yet, he was already there waiting for me in front. He didn't like being late.

"Billy!" I said when I saw him, my whole face alight in a triumphant smile.

He gave me a quick hug, took my hand, and pulled me inside. "They're crowded, and I need to get back to work. We'll talk in here."

But we couldn't, because as soon as we stepped in the door, I saw the whole Kohn family sitting at the center table. There was Sam, her husband, Mark, their children Sage and Willow, and there sitting next to Sage was—

"Mommy!" cried Aiden, who was—sitting next to Sage. "Daddy!" He jumped from his seat, wiped his hands on his napkins, ran over, and gave us both a big hug. "I missed you!"

"We missed you, too, buddy." Billy picked Aiden up and lifted him toward the ceiling. "Okay, now go back to eating your dinner."

"Lorry, Billy," said Sam. "Come on, join us." She moved over closer to Willow and Mark moved closer to Sage, leaving room for two chairs to squeeze in between them. Aiden sat between their two children.

Billy walked up to the counter to order for us, and I sat down next to Sam. "Good to see you, Sam. Hi, Mark."

"Lorry," Mark said and nodded.

"With these men and children in our lives, we hardly get together anymore!" said Sam.

I nodded and wished it was just me and Billy sitting at the table so I could tell him my good news. Then he could settle this and come home. Movement on the other side of the table caught my eye. Sage had his straw out of his glass and was about to blow the contents in Aiden's face. Aiden had a look of helplessness on his face. I was about to say something when Sam spoke up.

"Sage! You know better than that! Put the straw back in the glass or you won't get one next time! Come on, there's company. Be a mensch!"

Sage, looking unhappy, returned the straw to the glass.

"What's a mensch?" I asked. Sam always used Yiddish words I didn't understand. When I was in high school with her, I had learned quite a few but had forgotten them all over the years. So now Sam had to interpret for me.

"The literal translation means human being—also, a person of integrity and honor—but in this context, it means, 'act like an adult.'" I didn't have time to do much besides nod when Sam raised her voice again. "Willow! You need to act like a mensch, too." Then she leaned over to me and whispered loud enough for the whole table to hear, "Willow has a crush on Aiden."

Billy brought our food over, hamburgers and fries, sat down and started talking to Mark. Not that it mattered, because there was no way I could discuss the murder here at the table. Meanwhile, Aiden was mortified. He had heard Sam's whisper, and I could tell that he wanted to sink into the floor. And thus dinner moved on, with the children acting like children—not mensches —and the rest of us discussing nothing in particular and definitely not what I wanted to talk about.

When the Kohns finished, they packed everything up, including said children, uttered their goodbyes, and after Aiden hugged us one last time, they finally left Billy and I alone. I turned toward Billy, my face bright with anticipation.

Before I could speak, he started talking first. "I haven't told you an important part of the puzzle—one I've been trying to figure out all along. It doesn't make sense. I've never seen anything like it. Everybody, and I mean everybody, on the council including the mayor, had gunshot residue on them. The only ones who didn't were Martha and Russ Tabor and everyone in the audience, including you, Petra, Mason, and Todd Fenton."

"Oh," I replied, my high hopes of solving the crime dashed, or at least nearly dashed. There could still be an explanation for that, couldn't there? There had to be, because I knew I was right. I was, wasn't I?

Then Billy looked at his watch. "I have to go, Lor. I'm glad I got to spend a little time with you. Kind of with you!" He winked, and I knew what he meant. His quiet dinner for two had turned out differently from what either of us had expected. It was good to see Aiden, even briefly, but still. Billy stood up.

"Wait! I have to use the restroom. Can you wait a couple of minutes so I can walk out with you? Please?" Even though it looked doubtful, maybe there was an explanation for the weird gunshot residue results, and I was still right about Todd. I liked being right. Don't you?

"Yes, but hurry. I'll wait for you outside."

I finished my business as quickly as I could and as I headed through the restaurant toward the entrance, I noticed that Billy talking to someone outside. Lo and behold, you'll never guess who it was. Todd Fenton! What are the chances? Then something happened that blew my whole theory to kingdom come, wherever that is. Even farther than kingdom come, because a gunshot blasted through the air just missing guess who. Todd Fenton. At least it looked like it missed him. I thought he moved forward at the sound of the shot, but I was wrong.

CHAPTER FORTY-FIVE

IT DIDN'T MISS Todd; it got him right in the arm. There was blood all over. Was it Todd's or could the bullet have hit Billy, too? I did not let my three-inch heels stop me from running outside to make sure Billy was okay. He was already on the radio calling Nick for assistance. When he saw me, before I even had a chance to hug him and check for blood, he said, "Go inside and get some clean towels. An ambulance is coming."

Todd slunk to the pavement and leaned against the wall of Grizelda's. He held his hand over the hole in his arm as blood seeped through his fingers.

Running inside, I got the towels and raced back out. Billy didn't have to tell me what to do. I knelt down, eased Todd's hand away from his arm, placed a wadded-up towel on top of the wound, and held it firmly in place. Blood still gushed out. The bullet had gone clean through, so I put another towel on the back of his arm and put pressure on both, so he wouldn't lose so much blood. I think Todd would have scowled at me for my ministrations, but instead, his eyes disappeared in his head and his head lolled back against the building.

"Billy! I think he's going into shock!"

"Quick! Lay him down and elevate his feet!" Billy took off his coat and laid it on Todd.

I eased Todd onto the pavement and didn't know how I would elevate his feet. Since Billy sacrificed his coat, I would sacrifice my favorite dark blue dress and let Todd put his dirty boots in my lap. Yes, even *I* could sacrifice for the greater good, and right now, Todd needed the greater good. Before I could move down there—since I was still putting pressure on his arm wound—someone from Grizelda's came out the door with a big rock, that might have been used as a doorstop, and a couple of two by fours, and put those under his feet. Thank you. I was willing to ruin my dress but glad that I didn't have to.

"Lorry, stay here with him until the ambulance comes. It should only be a couple of minutes." And then Billy ran off in the direction the shot was fired. How did I know which direction that was? I saw the way Todd fell forward from the impact of the bullet. And I knew something else, too. The bullet was not meant for Billy. Whoever fired the gun had a clear shot at Billy and didn't take it. Normally at a time like this, I would say, *color me disappointed*, because I was wrong—again—about the killer. But I felt so happy Billy didn't get shot that I couldn't say that.

Todd moved and moaned under my pressure on his arm. Then he opened his eyes and looked around.

"Don't worry, Todd. The ambulance will be here in a minute. You'll be fine."

"What about Billy? Is he okay?"

What a strange thing to say, I thought. He must be deep in shock. I put my hand on his neck and felt his pulse. It was weak but there. "Yes, of course. *You're* the one who got hit."

Todd coughed. I half expected blood to come out his mouth, but he had gotten hit in the arm, not the lung. So none came out. "Billy got hit, too," he said. "The bullet went right through my arm and hit him. Not sure where. Is he okay?"

Looking down at the ground where Billy had been standing, I saw not one drop of blood. And when Todd had moved forward, he had moved right into Billy. But Billy get hit? Could it be true? I looked around to see who could take over for me putting pressure on Todd's arm, so I could go after Billy. Not only was there no one—well, there were plenty of people around, but no one who I would trust to do it—but Billy had told me to wait for the ambulance. When I agreed to that, though, I didn't know he could be wounded himself.

Still, I couldn't go traipsing around after Billy when someone was out there shooting people. That was stupid. Speaking of which, where was my purse? Glancing down, it hung from my shoulder where I had left it. At least I had the gun with me, but I still couldn't go after Billy. Just because I had a gun, didn't mean I knew how to use it. As much as I didn't want to stay there, I'd have to wait. "I *think* he's okay, Todd. I *hope* he is. I don't see any blood." My fear-tinged words tumbled out of my mouth.

"That's good," he said before closing his eyes again.

Looking anxiously in the direction Billy had run off, I saw no movement and had heard no more shots. That would probably be a good thing. I began to hear the ambulance in the distance coming closer. Briefly, I took the top cloth off Todd's wound. It wasn't bleeding as much as before. Either the pressure was working, or he was running out of blood to leak out. Not knowing which, I was grateful the ambulance got closer every second.

CHAPTER FORTY-SIX

THE AMBULANCE CAME and carted Todd off, saying they thought he would be okay and that I had done a good job staunching the flow of blood. I picked up Billy's jacket and looked down at myself. Miraculously, I had gotten no blood on either my jacket or my dress. I walked to my car and saw Billy's patrol car still parked there. So he's still wandering the streets searching for the shooter, I thought. The only natural course of action was to drive over to the Sheriff's Station to see if he'd called in.

They were probably getting tired of seeing me over there, but as long as bullets kept raining down on Rutledge, I needed to keep track of my new husband. Vanessa was nice as usual when I walked in there. "I've got a message for you, Lorry. Kind of, anyway."

"What do you mean, *kind of*?" I asked.

"Billy radioed in a cryptic message that I'm sure he meant for you. He said, 'Tell her I'm fine.' I know he's out looking for the shooter, but why would he say that?"

"The shot went right through Todd Fenton—"

"Wait. Todd Fenton, the guy whose father was killed?"

"Yes, same one. The bullet went through his arm and hit Billy. But I couldn't find any blood where he was standing. Still, I'm glad he told you he was okay. That makes me feel a little better."

Vanessa nodded. There had been no more bullets fired, so she didn't need to worry if her brother was okay, because he had been here, or somewhere else safe, when the first shot was fired. I wished Billy and Nick would walk in again as I stood there, but I had a feeling this would be a longer wait than the last time.

"Do you want to come back here and wait?" asked Vanessa.

"You know, I think I should go home. He said he was fine. Thank you for asking, though. I'll see ya later, Vanessa."

"Bye, Lorry."

Feeling dejected and more than a little scared, I walked out the door to my car. Bingo wagged his tail when I slid into the seat beside him. Leaning over, I kissed him on top of his head. "Daddy will be home soon, Bingo. I just know he will." I said it to make myself feel better, although I wasn't sure I believed it.

As I drove home, I looked down Church Street, and Billy's car was still there, but Billy was nowhere in sight. Sighing to myself and to Bingo, I drove home and pulled into the driveway behind Billy's truck—the one Mason and I would use the next day to move the boxes to the new house.

After changing clothes and heating up some leftover frozen pizza—my go-to meal when I was alone—and often when I wasn't, I knew I needed something to keep my mind occupied so I wouldn't worry about Billy. I tried one of Aiden's science documentaries, and that didn't help at all. So I decided since Mason was coming to help me move, I should get as many boxes packed as I could.

Billy had somehow dropped off more boxes between chasing killers, and this was a perfect time to fill them. And so I began. A couple of hours later as I sat on my butt admiring my handiwork, the phone rang. I raced up to get it, but it wasn't Billy.

It was Vanessa, though, with a message from Billy. The message was that *he was going to the hospital, but he was fine and was just going to see Todd Fenton. The bullet had luckily hit his bullet-proof vest and didn't cause his body any damage. He'd be home in a while. Don't worry and don't wait up.* But it was the last part of the message that I liked the best. He had told Vanessa to tell me *he loved me very much*. I thanked Vanessa and sat there in our office thanking the universe for bringing such a great guy into my life. It did much better than when it brought Eddie Keeley into my life, but I won't even go there. I'll feel grateful for what I have now.

Then I finished labeling and sealing all the boxes, so they'd be ready for Mason to load into the truck. Although I hoped Aiden would call, it didn't surprise me when he didn't. Not only had he called me earlier, but then we ended up eating dinner together.

And I didn't want to call over there acting like the over-protective mother that I was—because I didn't want to appear that way. Such is the life of a parent. I loved that life! As much as I wished Aiden was home with me, I understood Billy's concern that this murder had gotten personal. And I appreciated Billy being extra cautious with our son. Maybe he was over-protective, too? In this case, I think it was justified. Especially considering what happened next.

CHAPTER FORTY-SEVEN

KNOWING BILLY WOULD be home soon, I tried to stay up for him, but fell asleep on the couch instead. I knew Billy would understand. And he did. Even though he told me not to wait up for him, I think he appreciated it when I did. Next thing I knew he was sitting beside me on the couch, cuddling me, and telling me he was fine. Thank goodness. Maybe I was wrong about the direction of the bullet, and it really was meant for Billy.

"I'm home now, sweetie, and safe." He rocked me gently in his arms. "They were aiming at Todd, and the only reason I got hit at all, was because it went through Todd's arm. Look at this." Billy undid his shirt and showed me where the bullet hit the vest. "Another inch, and it would have hit me in the arm, too. This was a lucky shot, though." He shrugged. "Well, lucky for me, not so lucky for Todd, but he'll be fine."

"I'm so glad you're okay."

Billy shook his head. "No, I don't mean lucky that I'm okay. I think the person who did this aimed the gun so we couldn't find the bullet. Todd's back was an easy target—and bigger than his arm—but they wanted the bullet to go down the street never to be found. Since my body impeded its trajectory, I have the bullet! That's lucky! And it's safely delivered to Coyote Moon for ballistics. I put a rush on it. I should know tomorrow."

By that time, I was half asleep, and Billy helped me into the bedroom. Next thing I knew, it was morning. Billy kissed me good morning and goodbye at 6:30.

"Gotta run, hon. Good luck on the move with you and Mason. Today's the day I catch the killer! We'll celebrate tonight when I get home."

And he was off and I was back to sleep. Two hours later I woke up suddenly to a gunshot. It took me a minute to realize it was a dream. Still, it felt disturbing. Then I got frantic that Mason would be there any minute, and I wasn't ready. When I checked the clock, I still had more than an hour to shower, breakfast, and get dressed. And I could do it at my leisure, and so I did. With plenty of time before Mason arrived, I made myself fresh as a bouquet, dressed in my jeans and tennis shoes, and ready to move boxes.

The kitchen phone rang. "Hello! . . . Yes, Bryan, how are you? . . . I'm doing great! Billy and I are moving into a ranch! You and Ryan will be invited to the housewarming! . . . Oh! It's a done deal, really? . . . Everything I wanted? . . . You da man, Bryan! . . . Great. Thank you, and I'll let you know when the party is. . . . Bye!"

Bryan O'Keefe had perfectly handled all the lawyerly stuff I had given to him, as usual. Now everything was set.

Mason rang the doorbell at ten o'clock sharp, but he was in a glum and uncommunicative mood. "Hey, Lorry," he said when I opened the door, "let's do it."

"Is everything okay? Is Petra all right?"

"Everything is peachy-keen. Come on, let's get it done, so I can get back there."

After moving my car, I carried out the first box and opened the back door of Billy's truck to put it in there. Sliding the box onto the seat, I noticed a big, old leather suitcase. "What's this, Mason? I don't think it's Billy's."

"Hugo asked Petra to pack him a suitcase. With Petra at the bed and breakfast, he'll stay with Martha for as long as it takes."

"Billy said the case will be closed today."

"We can only hope," said Mason.

"Will Petra move back into her own home?"

Mason looked at me like I had insulted his manhood. With narrowed eyes, he gave me a curt reply. "Petra will *never* set foot in that house again." Then he turned away from me and marched into the house for another box.

His comment surprised me, but what surprised me more was his emphatic delivery. It shocked me. Petra didn't want to return to the house where her father committed suicide. That made perfect sense—except she hadn't wanted to go to the house even before that happened, which was why she was staying at the bed and breakfast to begin with. Nothing about the situation made much sense. But I followed Mason into the house, picked up another box, and forgot about it. We finished loading the truck in silence.

After we finished loading the truck, and Mason was about to back out of the driveway, I said, "Wait! I have to get my CCP purse or Billy will shoot me!"

I told Bingo to stay, and as I exited the truck, I heard Mason say, "Yeah, right."

When I returned to the truck, I patted the purse. "All set now." Then I placed the purse on the floor of the truck.

"What's a PPC purse and why is it so special?" asked Mason. "It looks like a regular purse to me."

What an innocent, I thought. Then I chided myself for being judgmental *again* because before a couple of days ago, I didn't know, either. "It's CCP. Concealed Carry Purse. It's got a gun in it. After Billy got shot at the other day, he said it's getting personal, so I should have a gun of my own. You know, just in case."

Mason glanced down at the purse and started the truck. "Whatever."

I chuckled. "Now you sound like me, Mason."

"Whatever," he repeated.

When we pulled out of the driveway, he said, "Nice truck," and he didn't speak another word until we reached the spot where I thought Hugo's car had been.

"I wonder what happened to Hugo's Cadillac."

"It's at your new ranch."

"How'd it get there and how do you know?"

"Billy and Nick came out, got it unstuck, and delivered it to your ranch. Billy mentioned it to Petra."

I shook my head. I'll never know how that man got everything done, plus his job, plus taking care of me and Aiden.

Mason stole a quick glance over at me and then moved his eyes back to the dirt road. "Lorry, I have to tell you something." Another quick glance at me. He was about to continue when I had to interrupt.

"Turn left here, Mason."

The moment passed and Mason didn't say another word until he asked which road to take when we drove through the gate and into the ranch. He took the middle road and pulled up into the driveway. "We're here," he said as he stepped out of the truck.

The first thing I noticed before I was even out of my seat was Charlie and his mangy dog coming out of the apartment on the other side of the garage. What was that man doing in there? I didn't trust him, I didn't, I didn't.

I was about to open my big mouth and tell him off when I heard Hugo say, "Mason, can you take the suitcase you brought me into the apartment over there? All of Martha's stuff is already in there. Charlie has been kind enough to bring it over there for us."

I slammed my mouth shut so fast and so hard that it made a noise and the mangy dog raised his head and gave me a dirty look. He probably growled, too, but I couldn't hear him. Charlie gave me a curt nod and walked by. When he got to Hugo and Martha, he shook hands with Hugo, exchanged a few words, gave Martha a kiss on the cheek, and then walked toward the bunkhouse in the barn with the dog following behind him.

Could I be wrong about the guy? No, I didn't think so. There was something about him besides being unsteady on his feet that day. Something I couldn't put my finger on. It was something he was hiding. I just knew it. Martha loved and was kind to everyone. And if Martha liked the guy, Hugo wouldn't argue.

Mason picked up the suitcase and toted it over to the apartment. I picked up a box from the backseat and carried it toward Martha and Hugo. Martha, since she couldn't hug me, kissed my cheek. By that time, Mason had delivered the suitcase and had another big box is in his arms. Martha followed him into the house.

I stood in front of Hugo, balancing the box on my hip. "You guys don't like the bedroom?"

"Oh, sweet Lorry! We love your bedroom! But it's *your* bedroom, and we don't want to impose any longer."

"Billy said he'll solve the case today, so it wouldn't be much longer."

Hugo's smile disappeared. He looked serious and leaned toward me whispering. "This whole episode has upset Martha so much that she has decided to take some time off. She's taking a leave of absence and may *never* return. I'm hoping she doesn't. But she also doesn't want to return to Rutledge for a while. Petra and her mother will run the bed and breakfast for now. So Billy said we could stay here in the apartment. You don't mind, do you?"

"No, of course not! You're welcome to stay as long as you want. You're family! Aiden will be thrilled!"

Mason came out then and without asking, took the box off my hip and carried it into the house. Martha emerged from the house, saying to Hugo as she walked by us, "I'll be in the apartment, straightening up."

Hugo watched her go and then put his hands on my shoulders and kissed my cheek. "I'll be right there, Martha!" He winked at me and followed her into the apartment. I heard him singing as he walked off, "You know that everything we share, so you must know I'll be right there!"

Mason and I finished unloading the boxes. Martha must have told him where everything belonged, because he dropped the boxes off in their respective locations and never said a word. The boxes were labeled, but he wouldn't have known where the rooms were without Martha's help. When we got back in the car, the first thing I did—after I patted Bingo—was make sure that Charlie man didn't steal my CCP purse. He didn't. It was still on the floor where I had left it.

CHAPTER FORTY-EIGHT

MASON STARTED THE truck and drove out the way we had come in. I hoped he would open up and tell me what he wanted to tell me before, but he didn't. He seemed fidgety but stayed silent. And so did I.

During the ride back on the rough road, my mouth stayed silent, but my mind zoomed in high gear reflecting on my suspect list. I wished that I had brought my notes with me. But I didn't realize that talkative Mason would suddenly become so taciturn.

After all my deductions and crossings out, I only had four people left on my list. And now I had to cross off Todd Fenton, because someone—presumably the murderer—had shot at him. I wondered if Billy had gotten the ballistics back yet and what it showed. But I couldn't call to ask. The last three people on my list were Brent Lindsay, Russ Tabor, and Christa.

Why was Christa even still on my list, I wondered. Then I remembered the conversation we had when she came into the historical society to visit. She asked some weird questions about the bullets. That was strange. When I thought back to the conversation, I concluded she was subtly, or not so subtly, pumping me for information. I knew that because I had done the same thing to other people. I was good at it, I thought, giving myself a virtual pat on the back.

Then there was Brent Lindsay. Why was he still on the list? Just because he broke off the conversation in mid stride? That's not enough. Some people were like that—not knowing how to make a polite exit. It bordered on rude, but it didn't make him a killer. I wouldn't cross him off, but I'd move him to the bottom of the list. My gut feeling was that it wasn't him—although I didn't have enough confidence to eliminate him from the suspect list.

Russ Tabor was probably my number one suspect right now. His being elevated to the town manager was proof he had something to gain. He had gained it. And now with Martha taking time off and possibly never going back meant that his nefarious scheme had worked. The town manager was a prestigious job. Rutledge may be a small town, but still, being the town manager was something. And being the town clerk was just another job. Russ's paycheck hadn't just gone up, his prestige and standing in the community had gone up, too. What do I call that? I call that motive. A strong motive.

And then I thought about the story Billy had told me regarding the gunshot residue. Everybody on the council had it on them, even the mayor who was not a suspect. He had been standing right in front of me when Fenton was shot. But Martha and Russ Tabor did not have it on them. Nothing about the whole scenario made any sense at all.

Then I remembered Elizabeth and Christa crying and hugging everyone. If it was one of them, the whole hugging and weeping scene could have been cover or trying to implicate everyone else. Perhaps I was too hasty taking Elizabeth off my list. Were they both crying? Both of them were doing the hugging. But who stood up first and started it? Was it Christa or Elizabeth?

Russ Tabor wasn't involved, so it couldn't have been him. That blows that theory. Was it one of the other men—supposedly to comfort the women? Brent Lindsay? As I pondered this, suddenly we were off the dirt road and on High Street, just a minute from home. My old home, that is. We had just left my new home.

As soon as Mason pulled into the driveway and turned off the truck, he jumped out. Bingo looked at him go, barked one quick bark, and stood up on my leg looking up into my face as if to say, "What are we waiting for?" I scooped him up and followed Mason into the house. He had unlocked the house with Billy's keys.

Mason was already in the office with the remaining boxes, but I was parched. "Mason, how about a cold drink before we continue? Come on, what d'ya say? I'm really thirsty."

"Lorry, I just want to get this over with." He carried out a box, saw me with my hands pressed together in front of my chest begging him, and he put the box down on the couch. "Oh, all right. What do you have?"

"Cola, lemonade, and iced tea." He had come up behind me, so I grabbed an iced tea and stepped away from the refrigerator. "Take your pick." As Mason pondered over the contents of the refrigerator, I heard a car door slam and a shout. I couldn't make out the words, so I walked over to the front window to look out and see what was going on. And that's when the proverbial poop hit the fan.

CHAPTER FORTY-NINE

IT WAS CHRISTA, and I wondered why she was at the house. I didn't even know she knew where we lived. After popping the top of the tea and taking a quick sip, I made my way to the door to open it and listen to what she was saying. My hand was on the handle, and I had pulled it open an inch when suddenly the door slammed shut, and Mason knocked me to the ground and was lying on top of me. "Mason!" I said. "It's *Christa.*"

Then a gunshot went through the door just over Mason's back. At least I hoped it went over his back. He didn't yell or anything. "Oh no, it's *Christa!*" That's when I figured it out. Christa's pumping me for information about the bullets and ballistics. *Christa* was the one who stood up first and started hugging. Now I knew that was to rub the gunshot residue off herself and onto everyone else. It was a smart move.

Mason reached up and locked the door, crawled off me, grabbed my hand, and pulled me so I was no longer in front of the door. "Quick! Where's your PPC purse?"

"CCP," I automatically corrected. "It's in the—" And I realized I had left it in the truck. "Oops."

"You don't have it? Oh, Lorry!"

Another bullet came sailing into the door and through it. "Wait! There's another gun in the bedroom. I don't know how to load the gun, but Billy said it had a magazine and was easy."

"Let's go!" Mason slithered on his belly toward the hallway and bedroom. "Come on! You can't stay there. Keep your head down!"

Following him down the hallway, I thought this was as good a time as any to tell him. "I don't know how to shoot it, Mason. Billy hasn't showed me yet."

"Just point it and pull the trigger. I'll do it. It's like a camera. Point and shoot."

"Yeah, right, Mason. You're going to be a doctor! Do no harm, and all that." Another bullet came through the door and lodged itself in the wall. My first thought as a sheriff's wife was Billy could easily retrieve that one for ballistics. As if it mattered at this point. Bingo was right behind me, crawling along like the rest of us.

Mason was already in the bedroom and now he turned around and spat out, "Lorry, Petra lost her virginity."

Still on my belly, I put my hands to my ears. "Mason, this is an awkward time to tell me about your sex life." Honestly, I thought in the stress of the situation he was losing it.

"Where's the purse?" he asked.

"The closet."

He stood up and in one fluid movement opened the sliding door of the closet, spotted the other CCP purse, pulled it down, and returned to the floor. Then he looked at me with fury in his eyes. "It wasn't *my* sex life!"

"Then who? Zack?" I asked in disbelief.

"No, of course not Zack! He's her *friend!*" He pulled the gun from the zippered pocket of the purse, looked at the magazine that Billy had already loaded, and slid it into the gun.

"Who else could it possibly—" And then I put it together: Petra coming in to work with her clothes askew. Petra staying at the bed and breakfast and not wanting to return to her house. Oh, no. Poor Petra. "That's probably why her father killed himself. He felt guilty about it."

"Oh, Lorry. Don't be so naïve," Mason said, clearly frustrated with me. He started creeping down the hallway toward the front.

A bullet shattered the front window glass. "Oh, no," I said. "Now she can crawl into the house through the window."

"I'll stop her." Mason moved from his stomach to his hands and knees toward the front window.

"Don't kill her! You won't be able to live with yourself." I told Bingo to stay and followed Mason out the door, skimming the floor with my big belly. Although I knew I'd be safer in the bedroom—more walls between me and the bullets—I needed to know the whole story. This time, curiosity could kill not the cat, but *the Lorry*, although I hoped not. It sounds stupid, but I couldn't help myself from following him out to the front room.

Without turning around to look at me, he said, "If I killed her, she wouldn't be the first, Lorry." Then he aimed the gun out the window and pulled the trigger. "Why do you think I spent most of yesterday in the bathroom? What I did made me sick to my stomach, but I don't regret it for a second." He looked down and shook his head, and I thought I might have seen a tear fall. "My Petra. Poor Petra."

That's when I understood what he meant by not being naïve. "Why didn't Petra call the authorities? They would have stopped him! Justice would have been served. *You* didn't have to kill him!"

After firing another bullet out the window, he turned to me with that horrible anger still covering his face. "Oh, really? Justice would be served? Like it was for Petra's brother? Like that, Lorry?"

That confused me. "But Petra's brother—"

"Committed suicide? Yes, that's right, Lorry. *Same as her father.*" Mason said as another bullet came through the open window. Mason fired back without looking out the window, as he had done before.

"But you said—" And then I realized what he meant. Someone had killed Petra's brother and made it look like suicide, just as Mason had done with Petra's father. "But who would—"

"The same person who just *committed suicide*."

"But Billy would never—" Then I calculated back to when Petra's brother died and realized it was before Billy became sheriff. "I can't imagine Wichita not figuring that out."

"It wasn't Billy or Wichita. It was that other sheriff."

Ah, yes, he meant the sheriff who was killed while on vacation in Chicago. "Oh," was all I said. It wasn't original, but it was all I could think of. Then something else occurred to me. "What a convenient coincidence that Petra's mother traveled out of town. You couldn't have done it if she was at home." I was putting everything together now, but I wanted to confirm that I was correct.

"Lorry, it *wasn't* a coincidence. That was the easy part. The bus ticket didn't cost me much and neither did the taxi ride to the airport."

Another bullet sailed over our heads. Christa, who had stopped yelling when she started shooting, began to speak. Since the window had no glass, we could hear her clearly.

"Lorry!" She yelled and paused like she was waiting for a response.

"Um, yes?" I said, hesitantly.

"You're probably wondering why I killed Christopher Fenton when I don't give a rat's patootie about the historical society building." She fired another shot into the door and then continued. "*Chris*," she spat out, "was my *intended*. We were to get married. I was *pregnant*. Then he up and drops the engagement. Turns out that the miserable jerk had gotten two women pregnant at the same time. He chose *her* over me. I've hated him ever since. And that's why I shot at his son. He should have been *my* son. But I didn't want to kill him, so I didn't. But I could have! Oh, yes. Make no mistake. I could have."

The whole thing shocked the stuffing out of me. I didn't know what to say but was glad Mason had the gun in case she tried to rush the house. Christa's voice sounded like she was still closer to the street than the house. Not that I felt at ease with a crazy woman shooting bullets into my house, but still—. Then I heard a siren. If Billy was coming to rescue me, he was almost too late. I was grateful he had made me buy a gun and even more grateful I had two.

"I did, though," Christa continued, "try to kill your husband, ole Billy Boy. It distressed me very much when I missed him. The uproar that would have ensued after his death would have been a perfect cover for me to get away with it. So, since I missed him, I figured I'd do the next best thing—*kill you!*" Just when I was beginning to relax, well, at least before she said she wanted to kill me, another bullet sailed into the open window.

"Do something, Mason! She wants to kill me!"

Then I heard Billy's patrol car pull to a stop outside. Mason poked his head above the bottom of the window. "Ah, oh."

"What? Billy's here. Everything will be okay."

"No. She's pointing the gun at Billy."

"Do something, Mason!" I yelled.

Mason's gun blasted, Christa screamed, and that was the last bullet fired.

"I'm sorry you had to kill her, Mason," I said, feeling bad for him, regardless of what he had confessed to me.

He grinned at me for the first time. "Lucky shot," he said. "I hit her in the gun arm and she dropped it." He stood up and pulled me by the hand to help me up. "See, Billy's got her handcuffed now. All is well. We're safe." He exhaled deeply. "And Petra's safe."

CHAPTER FIFTY

BILLY PUT CHRISTA in the back of his patrol car, and before he drove away, he blew me a kiss. Mason left, and I was alone with Bingo. Alone, shivering from head to foot. It took Bingo's wags and kisses thirty minutes before I calmed down. And all the while wind blew through the open window reminding me of the traumatic experience I had just experienced.

And the glass on the floor! Instead of cleaning up the mess, I sat there hugging Bingo and trying to forget what Christa had said about wanting to kill Billy. How many other perpetrators would want to kill Billy? What did I get myself into by marrying a *sheriff*? I sighed. There was nothing I could do. I was in love with him and would stay by his side no matter how many people shot at him. But I had to admit if Christa were the last one, I wouldn't mind at all. Instead of focusing on the fear and the horror of people shooting at Billy, I would focus on the gratitude I felt that he was such a good husband to me and a good father to Aiden. And I would leave it at that.

Time passed with me gulping deep breaths trying to come to terms with what had happened. The gunshots. My new gun. Mason shooting at Christa. Mason's confession. The discovery of why Petra had been acting so unlike herself. All of it unsettled me. I don't know how long I sat there pondering before the glass fix-it guys knocked on the door. Billy must have called them. They measured how big a piece of glass they needed to fix the window, and then they boarded it up with plywood, saying they would bring the glass on Monday.

When they left, it prompted me into action. I walked to the kitchen, called Bryan, and told him the new project I needed done. Then I realized I had promised Mason pizza, but hadn't come through with it. So I ordered the pizza and asked how long it would be before they delivered it to the bed and breakfast. And since I figured we were done moving for the day, I changed out of the jeans and tennis shoes and put on a long blue skirt, matching blue top, and my brand new high-heeled cowboy boots. I needed to break them in so I wouldn't get a blister. Today was as good a day as any. And I loaded Bingo into the car and drove over to Martha's bed and breakfast.

I arrived at the same time as the pizza, paid them the money, added a big tip for delivering it still steaming hot, and carried it inside with Bingo following. My CCP purse was over my arm—I wouldn't leave that sucker behind again—I had learned my lesson.

Mason was the first one to spot me from the top of the stairs. "You came through! I thought you were too upset over what happened to even remember! What a gal, Lorry, what a gal! Petra! Pizza!" Then he came bounding down the stairs, licking his lips. Maybe he wasn't licking his lips, but it sounded good.

Although I had bought enough pizza for the English guests who were staying there, Mason informed me they had already left, so we set the table in the small kitchen instead of in the dining room. Petra arrived in the kitchen as we opened the pizza box and started divvying it up.

"Just in time, Petra! Dig in!"

"Lorry! Did you hear?" It was the most animated I had seen her all week.

"Hear? What are you talking about, Petra? I was there! Mason must have told you!"

Petra put her hand in front of her stuffed mouth and waved what I said away. "No, no. I'm not talking about that. I'm talking about the historical society! It got sold! But it was to somebody else, not Fenton. Somebody paid big bucks for it, and even Fenton couldn't match it."

I said, "Hmmm," and kept chewing.

"So I don't know if we should worry about our jobs or not. Maybe that person is planning on tearing it down like Fenton was."

"Tear it down? I thought they were going to make it into an indoor mall or something."

"That was the rumor they spread before they put in to buy it. They were going to raze it."

"The thought of that makes me sick to my stomach," I said and meant it.

"I know. So I'm hoping they won't do that. But I am concerned about my job. Now that my dad is gone, I need to keep working."

"I thought you and your mom were going to stay here and run the place."

"We are. My mom will get paid, but for me, it will just be a place to live. And I don't think we'll make enough money on the sale of the house for any savings at all. My father kept taking second and third mortgages on it."

And not to mention he let the place get run down into the ground. They would have to sell it as a fixer-upper. Petra was right. They probably wouldn't make any money on it at all. They may even end up owing money, depending on the financial state her father had left them in. I doubted her father had any life insurance, and I wasn't going to ask. Instead, I said, "I'm sure everything will work out fine, Petra."

Petra wanted to know what happened, even though Mason had already told her the whole story. So I described everything, and it matched Mason's account. He kept looking at me while I talked, probably wondering if I would tell Petra his confession about her father. If Petra was to know about that, he would have to be the one to tell her. When I finished the story, Mason looked relieved. The pizza was almost gone, and it was time for me and Bingo to return home.

Billy got home late afternoon looking exhausted. He had worked a ton of hours this week. But at least he got the killer before she killed one of us. When I heard him pull up with his patrol car, I met him as he came inside the house. I'm not sure which one of us was holding the other tighter, me or him. We had both been in danger of getting killed on this one. It took a long time of tight hugging before we released each other.

"I love you so much, and I'm so glad you're safe," he said.

Looking up at him, all I could think to say was, "Ditto." And then I started sobbing. After Billy calmed me down, I asked, "How did you know it was Christa?"

"Russ Tabor admitted he didn't see her coming out of the restroom. He lied because he was sneaking in from smoking outside and didn't want his wife to find out. That blew Christa's alibi. And the weird results for the gunshot residue kept preying on my mind. When I questioned Elizabeth again, she remembered that Christa was the one who started the hugging. That clinched it. And when I heard the gunshots coming from the direction of home, I figured you were in the middle of it *yet again*."

After we talked about Christa's prior relationship with Christopher Fenton, I said, "Interesting that I thought it had to do with the historical society sale, but it was really secrets for sale."

We spent most of what was left of the afternoon on the couch in each other's arms and said nothing more about the murder. The situation had scared both of us, and we were both grateful the other had survived. Billy had eaten while he was out and about, and I was stuffed with pizza, so we each had a sandwich and not too long after that decided to retire early.

We lay there in silence for a long time, comforted by being in each other's arms. Then Billy said, "I got the ballistics back on Petra's father's gun."

I didn't know if he suspected foul play or not, but I wasn't going to say anything. "Oh?" I tried to sound ignorant about the guy's death. Billy and Mason were close.

"Yes, it matched another crime of several years back during the term of that sheriff killed in Chicago. You've probably heard the rumors. Petra's brother. It was set up to look like suicide, but it wasn't. The sheriff couldn't find any evidence to the contrary, but I don't know how hard he tried. Petra's brother was murdered. It wasn't suicide. And funny how it was the same gun found at Petra's father's bedside."

Where was he going with this, I wondered. Did he suspect Mason? Would he arrest him?

Then Billy gave me the answer I wanted.

"But justice was served."

Billy knew. And Mason wouldn't be arrested—because justice was served.

If you liked this book and feel so inclined, please leave a review on Amazon. Thank you! I appreciate it!

And if you'd like to know when the next Rutledge Historical Society mystery comes out, sign up for the mailing list: http://www.ralstonstorepublishing.com/mysteryL.html

Read the next book in the series: Lady Smith Lady.

When a stranger is murdered at their new ranch, Lorry feels compelled to join in the investigation, much to Billy's dismay.

Other books published by Ralston Store Publishing:

Time Travel Sweet Romance
Cowgirls in Time Series by Erica Einhorn
A Chill Wind
Wind Beneath My Wings
Against the Wind
The Healing Wind
Ride Like the Wind
Wind of Change
The Way the Wind Blows

Caregiving
The Journey that Matters by Jodie Lightener

Suspense
Darkness in the Light by J.K. Lincoln

India
Not My Guru by Parvati Hill

Women's Fiction/Reincarnation
Two Lifetimes, One Love by Thea Thaxton

Yoga Books
Bathroom Yoga
Airplane Yoga
Wheelchair Yoga
Essential Yoga on Horseback
Exercises for Therapeutic Riding   >>>>>>>>>>>>

JK's Self-Publishing Guides

JK's Quick Start Guide to Scrivener (Windows)

JK's Quick Start Guide to Selling Books Through Amazon KDP

JK's Quick Start Guide to Amazon Ads Marketing

JK's Quick Start Guide to Selling Books Through Ingram Sparks

JK's Quick Start Guide to Copyrighting Your Book

www.ingramcontent.com/pod-product-compliance
Lightning Source LLC
Chambersburg PA
CBHW051502170626
46811CB00002B/595